ZARDOZ

T0182425

JOHN BOORMAN

WITH BILL STAIR

BASED ON THE
ORIGINAL SCREENPLAY
BY
JOHN BOORMAN

Published by Repeater Books

An imprint of Watkins Media Ltd

Unit 11 Shepperton House

89-93 Shepperton Road

London

N1 3DF

United Kingdom

www.repeaterbooks.com

A Repeater Books paperback original 2024

1

Distributed in the United States by Random House, Inc., New York.

ISBN: 9781915998521

Ebook ISBN: 9781915672629

Printed and bound by CPI Group (UK) Ltd, Croydon, CR0 4YY

CONTENTS

PREFACE TO THE 1974 EDITION

I wrote *Zardoz* in 1972 at my home, a lost valley in the dreaming hills of Wicklow. It came out closer to a novel than a screenplay. Gradually I worked it into a film form that proved too radical for most of the studios. Finally I got some backing and shot the movie in our local studios, Ardmore, and locations around my house between May and July, 1973.

In the final weeks of preparation, Bill Stair – who worked with me on *Point Blank* and *Leo the Last* – came in to help rationalize the visions that threatened to engulf me.

While editing the film I decided to restore the story to novel form. I asked Stair to help me with it. It follows the film very closely but draws heavily on the earlier versions. It offers an interpretation of the film and helps to lay to rest those ghosts that stalked the Celtic twilight pressing this strange vision of the future upon me.

John Boorman, September 1973

PREFACE TO THE 2024 EDITION

I wrote this book alongside making the film *Zardoz* in 1974. The film has become something of a cult, with followers all over the world. How did the idea come into my head? I was observing how the poor get poorer and the rich get richer and how the well-off are living longer and healthier lives than the poorest. I propelled these tendencies into a future in which the beautiful people live eternal lives and largely ignore the sufferings of the world outside – until a character called Zed comes along and penetrates their enclave, wreaking havoc with the strictly measured lives of these "Eternals." To pacify the people of the outside world they invented a God – Zardoz – a flying head which issues laws and instructions to the common people, who readily obey his words. In one scene towards the end, there is a line spoken by Connery: two of the characters are boasting about the flying head and its effect on simple folk, and Zed responds by saying, "I have looked into the face of the force that puts the idea in your mind; you are bred and led yourself!" Some of Zardoz's admirers have latched onto that speech as a foundation of religion.

In *Zardoz*, the overwhelming question is why we have to die, and this would urge the kind of society as imagined in the book and film. Once this has been addressed, there is the question of living forever, and all the questions that come after it. The Eternals turn nature on its head and deny that we all belong to it, that we all die and rot away like the best of flowers. Do we dare challenge that law? Essentially, *Zardoz* is about a group of scientists who do defy nature and fundamentally set themselves up as distinct from nature, where everything grows and flourishes and dies, which unfortunately includes the human species. Once you take the step out of nature, you do so at your peril – those are the thoughts that were also in my head as I wrote *Zardoz*.

John Boorman, March 2024

ZARDOZ

PROLOGUE

"We seal ourselves herewith into this place of learning. Death is banished forever. I direct that the Tabernacle erase from us all memories of its construction, so we may never destroy it if we should ever crave for death. Here man and the sum of his knowledge will never die but go forward to perfection."

The old man finished speaking. There was no applause from the assembled audience. They quietly dispersed and went about their allotted duties.

Eternal Life had begun.

CHAPTER ONE

Zardoz Speaks

Nothing was easy. Life came hard and short. The young boy, Zed, took shelter at the side of his father from the merciless wind. They were fortunate, they were the blessed ones. They waited at the mountaintop.

Others were gathering on horseback. All moving to the appointed place, all heads turned to the point on the horizon from whence Zardoz would come.

Zed's sharp eyes swept the bare landscape. Acres of hook-thorned shrubs jostled in the unceasing wind, their dry leaves whispering across the tundra. Low tussocks of gray grass gave way to deformed woods and midget oaks that rose from pools of brackish, oily water – and all the plants were dead.

First there was a low note, then one of the watchers pointed to the heavens. A shout rose up. "Zardoz comes!"

Through the lowering clouds came their God. This was to be the first time that Zed would see him. Even he, a warrior's son, shook with fear and fell to his knees when he saw God.

A gigantic stone head slowly descended toward them. Vast and menacing, its huge face was carved into a frightening grimace, its eyes glowing, its face glittering with rain. How could a head live without a body? What kind of creature could have borne this monster? Perhaps the body was invisible and all around them. Zed stood firm. The warriors raised a huge salute as the head came to rest before them on the hilltop.

Zed was privileged. His father had the right to slay and breed, and these would be his rights too. He could take women in the name of Zardoz, and he could kill in that name. He would be One with Zardoz, he would be a Man.

"Zardoz speaks to you his chosen ones."

The earth trembled with the voice. The warriors replied, "We are the chosen ones," their eyes averted. Zed dared raise his head and look into the black mouth of Zardoz, into the dazzling, molten eyes.

"You have been raised up from brutality to kill the Brutals who multiply and are legion. To this end Zardoz your God gave you the gift of the Gun."

High above the head appeared a hand, then in the hand a gun. So real was the dream that Zed reached out to touch it, but the giant thumb pulled back the hammer and the forefinger squeezed the trigger and the gun fired. The report exceeded even the noise of Zardoz's voice. The Gun!

Another part of the litany familiar to all the congregation except Zed; to him the miracle of the firing vision was only exceeded by the next image.

"The Gun is good," boomed Zardoz.

"The Gun is good," repeated the warriors.

"The penis is evil. The penis shoots seeds and makes new life to poison the Earth with a plague of men, as once it was. But the gun shoots death and purifies the Earth of the filth of Brutals. Go forth and kill. Zardoz has spoken."

Before Zed's startled gaze the God vomited up thousands of weapons; guns, swords, bullets, rifles, all spewing out of his mouth onto the hillside. The Exterminators, the killers of the Brutals, surged forward, forgetting their fear of the huge God. They fought for the weapons and gave thanks to Zardoz for his bounty. Zed had run forward too, had claimed his first weapon, a revolver, and was now a man, a warrior, a priest of Zardoz.

Zed lived with his father in an encampment at a hilltop.

It flattened into a wide plateau and bore signs of other times and other men. High earthen walls rose above deep ditches that grew with spiked stakes, impaling rotting heads of slaughtered Brutals. Guards strolled the walls, and called the names of those who rode up to the gateways, always friends returning, never foes. The gates led to an intersection around which grew the camp. A profusion of many-shaped shelters, of cloth, skins, metal, and wood, all smoking and begrimed, surrounded the long hut of the warriors. This stood tall like an upturned boat beached in the center of the flotsam of the hovels at its rim.

The women and children were quartered in these surrounding places. They were of a slave-rank, the adult females captured in raids, chosen for their strength and the features prescribed by Zardoz. His shrine was at the head of the long house. Here the men lived, for the most part in seclusion. Cooking fires drifted smoke up from the holes in the rooftops. A stockade of pigs was by the walls. The children, if males, were taken from their mothers at an early age and trained in all the martial arts. The females became, as their mothers, chattels and slaves of the camp. Life was drear for them. Each warrior had as many wives as his station could support. As a warlord, Zed's father had many. If Zed was strong enough he too would warrant many wives and concubines. He too could be the paramount chieftain of the hill.

Zed became a zealous soldier and fearless fighter in the name of Zardoz. A great Crusader in his name. He killed and grew and in the growing multiplied his deaths. He was, like Zardoz, insatiable. When he took women, it was in the same mad lust in which he slaughtered. The only meaning of his life was to be found in the service of Zardoz, in absolute obedience to the one and only force. For had not this God given him the right to mate, the means to kill? What else could there be that was meaningful? Zardoz made him, and Zed was a willing instrument of that will. As the years passed, he became, as his father had become, the leader, the archpriest, the knight-supreme of the holy order.

Upon their war-horses they were one with the beasts they rode. Bridled and saddled with red leather, the Exterminators rattled with old trophies, scalps, fingers, bone, rings, and trinkets from the dead. Paint zigzagged on the legs of the horses, dazzling the eye when they galloped.

The warriors sat tall in the saddle, moustaches drooping below their chins, long hair sometimes tied back, or knotted atop their heads and set with long bone pins. To strike fear in the hearts of Brutals, they wore red masks in the image of Zardoz.

Zed was more starkly dressed. His long hair was tied back, a moustache dark against his swarthy skin, a leader who scorned finery and decoration. His huge horse was as blue-black and glittering as his hair, fleet as raven's wings.

Zed wore long boots that rose up to his thigh tops, a breechclout, and swathes of encircling ammunition belts across chest and waist. A rifle hung in a bucket holster at his saddle bow, a long six-shooting revolver sat high on his right hip, and a saber was scabbarded at the saddle. His hand gripped a slender steel-tipped lance from which fluttered a red pennant. Blood-red like all they wore, but casting a black and deadly silhouette against the sun.

After each full moon, they would gather to do homage to their king. They would offer up live sacrifices, a few fortunate Brutals who would be lucky enough to see the Mighty One before death came. Then they would receive new supplies with which to carry on their unending campaign of carnage. Revitalized and renewed they would return to their duties.

He had to ride many miles in his search, through strange dead forests, through weird places where once many Brutals dwelt, encampments that had long borne the scars of the Exterminators. And at other times, the hooves of their horses rang on stone. They chased the dead and dying through strange free-standing caverns, empty for ages. Zed knew no fear for, although it was said these buildings were haunted, indeed cursed, by the spirits of the long-dead giants that had built these ingenious dwellings, he knew that Zardoz was always by his side.

No fear, no compassion ever crossed his mind, for he knew that he was but a vehicle, the angel of death, inspired by Zardoz.

In killing, as in the final moment in the act of love, he was supreme. That was his purpose. For he knew that he was but an instrument of the Almighty, the Unmerciful, the All-Seeing.

Many roads were ridden in the cause of Zardoz, many routes crossed and recrossed, through the traces of the old times that were still left, and out into the barren lands beyond. Often his sword rose and fell in the cause; many times his guns roared death and confusion on the subhuman host that ran below the hooves of his war-horse. They were a ghastly and awful host that fell to his sword, so unlike his followers as to seem a different breed. Some ran on monstrous distorted limbs, were many-headed; some slithered; others, eyeless, sensed his presence with antennae; still more gazed at him with red and green eyes, mottled skins blending them with the earth. These were not men, and yet they all echoed that frame.

He rode relentlessly over the dead-lands, taking little rest, for everything was to be reduced and smitten. From this sterile loam some evil life eked out, clinging as life will in its most perverse extremity. A slime lived on the trees, a many-legged worm burrowed through the soil and sucked life from the slime, long-tusked pigs dug for sustenance in the dead copses and found enough strength in the worm-bodies to kill any man on foot. These boars fed larger life – great cats and dogs and bears and man himself – while over all the wasteland vultures flew, waiting.

All the life, whether it crawled, dug, buzzed, or flew upon the earth, was dark as the dust – except for subman. He was sallow but still not blackened by the poisonous pigment. The world was to become as Zardoz wished. The model was the sterile, ashen wastes over which the exterminating horde swept; where the black earth crumbled underfoot. Everything was to be as Zardoz ordained: empty, bleak, and dead, except for the warriors who would ride out forever on the black wastelands of their God. This had to be accomplished, for Zardoz had so ordered things. The hammer of his will was the Exterminators, the Brutals were the anvil, the ragged remnants of that which had once encompassed the Earth and engulfed it... humanity.

Zed was mighty. None was more zealous in the praise of God nor more talented in carrying out his will. His wisdom outshone the others, no eye was truer, no arm stronger, no mind mightier. The others feared his thoughts more than the man himself. Zed himself was pursued by constant dreams. He saw things that were not visible.

He could have been driven from the tribe and killed as an evil spirit were it not for his proven greatness as a warlord. His sword and gun were the most potent of the group; did this not demonstrate that he was possessed by Zardoz? The powers of the God himself? Zed's following grew, no other groups of killers could match him. None could exceed his harvest. And then it was that Zed found there were others like him.

Only a few; three other warlords like himself. They met at a gathering of the tribes. He recognized they were all brothers in intellect and intuition. Few words were spoken but their hands were joined briefly, in a lasting bond of more than friendship. He was not alone, these were brothers in mind and spirit. Even as a superior son of Zardoz, he had indeed found kindred fellows. These were not only soldiers, they had the same strange and frightening powers as Zed. Their intellect outshone their physical prowess.

As Zed grew and formed his inner circle of brothers, so Zardoz grew. The mighty God, no less deadly, began to temper his edicts with a new wisdom. Zed was disturbed, but dissolved his doubts in his passion for obedience. The new orders concerned growth. Just as Zed himself and a special few could breed, so Zardoz gave a new seed to the landscape. Zardoz commanded that prisoners be taken, not to be sacrificed in his name, but to work, to plant the soil, to grow grain.

Disgusting as it was distasteful, Zed was obedient. The slaves planted the soil with grain that came from Zardoz's mouth and in time that grain grew and multiplied, was reaped and then returned to the mouth from which it came, the jaws of Zardoz. Crops would not grow in the sour soil but Zardoz gave them new seeds, proof against the poisons of the blighted earth.

Zardoz demanded food, demanded grain, and still delivered weapons for the unending but changing fight against the Brutals. Now, however, prisoners were to be taken with the net and rope. Only a few could be killed, in ritual reenactments of the old times. Zardoz was Mighty, Unending, Unanswerable. Zed, for all his passionate belief, felt strange doubts, as did his newfound brothers.

In the acts of worship – the capture, the kill – Zed now felt uncertainty.

Dare he talk to the others? Dare he share his doubts?

As he stood before the mighty head, as he had many times before, stunned as ever by the presence and the might of Zardoz, he heard a whisper from within his skull that Zardoz was not all he seemed but less, and more, than the stone face which faced him now. Much time would pass before Zed could unravel the fears and questions that were rising in his mind; clues and help would come from unexpected quarters... there would be time... there would be times.

CHAPTER TWO

The Cavern

At first it was a rustling, then it was a dry sifting sound, and then low like rain, liquid but insistent.

Zed could hear again. His eyes opened and he was surrounded by blackness. His mouth opened but he could make no cry. He was suffocating, drowning, deep inside a well. He struggled. His arms slid smoothly through the granules that pressed him down. His gun arm pushed through into clear air above. The gun rose first, pulling the arm and body up into life again.

As the seeds that had surrounded him cascaded from his body, Zed found himself within a stone vault, domed, ancient, and glittering. It was lit by the sparkling glow of two orbs. The corn still spattered from him as he turned to view the interior that had swallowed him. His eyes became accustomed to the darkness, and forms grew from the light and dark. Above him, rank on rank, stood chrysalis-like forms; beneath them, worn stone steps tumbled down to where he stood.

Between him and them were littered piles of produce from the land: corn, root-crops, fleeces.

The entrance to the cavern, a low, rough-hewn long doorway, was not far from him. Outside clouds and mist were scudding by. He was adrift, floating through the air in the flying stone head of Zardoz. He had entered the mouth like a morsel of food and now stood like some errant thought within the brain space of the monstrous head.

And on the wall near him was a handprint. Man was here. It was a sign, a signature of authorship.

Quickly climbing up the stone steps he moved toward the figures above him. The walls were cold and damp and glistened with sparkling lights. The light from the two illuminated globes gleamed off the stone as he passed. Rainbow pools of light danced before his eyes as he steadily walked upward, his gun leading. At the top, his path was blocked. Rows of blank, unseeing naked bodies gazed out through huge fetal sacs. They were neither alive nor dead, though all bore marks of violence. They seemed to guard the vast cave. Were they bodies saved from some battle? Had he himself been among them and escaped? His mind was not yet steady.

He passed by these blind apparitions to the circles of light, and gazing through the cracked and shining transparencies, he perceived a landscape, miles below.

A moving landscape. He was flying, moving slowly through the air above the barren, desolated earth he had helped create. Lost in the wonder of this picture he failed to hear the first footfall settle below and behind him, but turned before the second one had fallen. Looking down, he saw a figure moving to the cavern entrance directly beneath where he stood.

Zed turned, jumped, and landed catlike behind the figure who now stood nonchalantly leaning on the top lip of the narrow entrance, gazing down as Zed had done a moment before, looking at the passing of a fragmented, ruined city. The man turned and looked at Zed as if he had expected him, not alarmed, animate but serene. A plump, round face with a small beard below merry, sparkling eyes. Like the people in the transparent sacs above, he had an awesome disdain that cut through the bearded grin. He wore his strange and colorful clothes as if for inspection by a lesser being; condescendingly, casually. He had the look of a man who might vanish, or turn into a mischievous spirit; alien, elaborate, and deadly. And, overall, the frightening and persistent look of one who is assured to a point of unnatural supremacy.

Zed was unafraid; his gun floated up effortlessly to confront the smiling face. He fired. The body took the bullet well, barely moving as the metal passed clean through. It buckled slightly as the truth transmitted to its brain.

The head turned back to Zed; to plead perhaps?

"You! How foolish. I could have shown you... without me... you are nothing... so pointless."

He laughed and fell. Caught in the slipstream, he hung for a moment. "How pointless!" he cried again. He danced one moment longer on thin air and then was lost without a cry.

Zed saw him fall like a brilliant dart into the clouds below, his cloak still fluttering gaily as if in mockery of his death.

CHAPTER THREE

The Vortex As Heaven

Zed still stood in the mouth, leaning against the upper teeth, mirroring the last position of his victim. Zed had taken the place of that body in more ways than one. He was the only aware being on the flying craft, all the rest were as dead, or about to be dead. He smiled at the thought.

He looked down with something of the triumph the man had earlier showed to him.

Zed allowed himself a faint smile. Things were progressing favorably. He still lived.

He let the wind whip at his clothing and the light rain beat against him. It ran from his body as it ran from the surface of the flying vehicle.

As it ran down Zed's lips so it ran down the curved lips of Zardoz, and Zed looked out from that awful mouth-doorway, a minute figure. The gaping mouth, the glaring eyes floated serenely on, but they contained a new commander, Zed. Through the glowing orbs which had so frightened Zed as a boy, youth, and man, Zed looked down upon the cities of which he had been so afraid. Zed had pierced the God head. He was inside the hollow shell he had once so revered. From whence or how it moved, he knew not, but that it was false he was certain. The love and reverence with which Zardoz had once filled him could no longer protect him, for he had found that his God was hollow as this ship. He was alone. His quest had begun.

The head floated on, gradually descending through the clouds into a valley cradling a lake. A fertile, green oasis in a black land. He flew lower and lower over fields that pleased him with their verdant exactness. Carefully laid paths and canals crisscrossed the neatly tilled land. Rows of fruit-bearing trees led the way downward. A profusion of blossom and color rose up to greet the head. The head circled slowly as if searching for a gap in an invisible wall, as if the valley were protected by more than high cliffs and mountains.

It sank down toward a cluster of dwellings, strange and elegant yet archaic. Zed did not look down on them; he had reburied himself in the grain at the center of the head.

With a strange hiss like the sighs of a thousand voices the head came to rest. Zed waited a moment, then ran to the mouth, leaped through, tumbled down the stony beard, and ran for cover as fast as his lightning reflexes and strong muscles would take him. There was no moment to look and wonder. He just had time to run, leap, and hide. The head had come to rest in a cluster of farm buildings, its mouth facing inward on to a courtyard, its eyes glaring down at the rooftops.

Gun first, he probed into the building in whose doorway he had sheltered. A strange and dusty interior. White dust everywhere. Long cones poured more dust into sacks. The smell of baking filled the air. Zed crept quietly along rows of freshly made loaves. He reached and picked one up, and as the mill ground corn into flour, the flour was mixed and cooked, all by some unseen hand. Zed tasted food for the first time in many days.

Only a bite, a taste. The bread was green. Bread – a

slave food; green magic! He touched the floury surface. He scanned the room as a hunter, detached and quick. The next moment he left the bakery to continue its automatic way. Almost soundlessly, he left as he had entered.

Zed was once again in a courtyard. The head had come to rest outside, the bakery was behind him. To his right, another building seemed to call him. It was a cottage, with two distended transparent domes in front of it, bulging breast-like, filled with plants.

Intrigued, Zed approached cautiously. On the roof were delicate silver vanes, turning into the sun, following its rays like flowers. Inside the cottage Zed gently prodded the dome doorways; they parted like lips.

Zed was within a womb of foliage that itself contained many other transparent buds and growth points for infant plants. They lived in membranes that swelled and grew from floor to ceiling, each attached by tubings to other plants and sources of nourishment.

The wet earth in troughs crawled with life, teeming with worms and soft, many-legged insects. A rotting sweet stench of decomposition pervaded all. The moist air seemed to close around him, condensing on his body. Vivid blossoms hung before him. He brushed against thick leaves that seemed fashioned by a demon's hand rather than grown from the soil. Spiky thorns clutched at him as he passed. Spheres within spheres contained other, greener growths wreathed in moist fogs.

Slime begat gases and nutrients for plants which in turn fed larger, stranger breeds, fulfilling some subtle biological plan. Seasons stretched on or speeded by in other tanks and casks.

Familiar wheat plants basked in unearthly violet lights

while their naked roots floated in clear liquid. Some grain plants were monstrously tall, others fat and sleek with grass stems. The whole, a green menagerie of the exotic and half real, a universe in which he was the alien. All this was in step with a purpose. He was a lone mammal, adrift in their land. Notwithstanding this, there was human presence overall. The fine-tuned tubing, the delicately calibrated vessels, the scales, the bright bags of colored dusts, the clean and neat arrangement of the place – it all be-spoke a planner. All was complex and interwoven, yet it had been conceived and ordered. The lush vegetation was the result of countless plans and progresses – where was the creator of all this life?

Zed was enfolded and lost within the slippery midget forest of glass and plants. Its humid air oppressive, he groped for a door – an exit into air. He felt the walls, sniffing like a dog for its prey. He sensed his quarry lurked here. In some seclusion deeper than this, beyond these walls yet near at hand, was the man who had made all that.

His hands ran over the walls, searching. His cunning fingers found a crack. He pushed and a door creaked open, revealing a flight of steps. His hunter's skill was bearing fruit.

The new room was quite different from the first. It was a jumble of strange bits and pieces, yet it seemed to have a life, a happier purpose than the places below. Drawings, plans, and toys were cluttered and crammed into the attic of the cottage. Zed picked up one box, and opening it, jumped back as a tiny toy popped out at him then hung, limply suspended. Was it all a complex joke? Were they all in one vast game? He walked through a beaded curtain into another room, velvet curtains enclosed a painting – Zardoz! Zed leaped back as if discovered. Could Zardoz still see him? Was the God alive?

"Attention, attention, attention!"

Zed felt that he was not yet discovered, but knew the voice was near. It came from a mirrored box. Opening it, he saw a ring with a crystal stone. It was glowing with an inner light and the voice issued from it.

"Harvest produce report, submit surpluses and needs for inter-Vortex barter and exchange, year 2293, third harvest yield."

As Zed toyed with the ring, figures began to float in the air before him, in red and green and white.

He reached out to touch them, remembering how he had tried to touch the gun of Zardoz in the same manner when a boy. The figures vanished and reappeared in ascending and descending order. Soap, leather, salt, barley, oats. The surplus of one Vortex could pass to another which had need of it. Numbers passed from one section to another. And all in midair, issuing from the ring. He moved his hand and caught the figures on his palm, compressing them down until one hand covered the other. He sent the images spiraling and shooting around the room. Then they vanished, and the air was still. Hunger pulled at him. His fast had been long.

"Meat," he mumbled.

Meat appeared in midair, transparent but real. An image in thin air. He spoke again.

He could look into the ring and see the image still. He could project it onto the walls. He could command it.

"Who lives here?"

The face of the man he had killed in the flying head's mouth appeared before him.

"I am Arthur Frayn – Vortex Four."

"No!" How could this man come back to haunt him, to betray him? The face grew huge, until only a single eye filled the wall. It cartwheeled across the ceiling as Zed's hand shook.

"I am Arthur Frayn, Vortex Four. I am Arthur Frayn, Vortex Four."

The accusing voice continued, unhindered, remorseless, in its calm insistence, a mocking denial of its own death. Zed shook with fear, there was no end to this repeating answer. Zed's question had begun an endless comment on his murderous action. He shook the ring, stamped on it, shouted for it to stop, but the voice droned on as if to drive him mad. In desperation he stuffed the ring under a cushion, to suffocate the image. But soon the voice came from under there, muffled but distinct.

"I am Arthur Frayn, Vortex Four..."

Zed was startled by newer voices, from outside the walls. Moving to the window he looked down and saw people unloading the Zardoz head of its membrane-covered bodies. They were all young and lovely. They carelessly threw the bodies onto wooden carts. One girl counted them off.

"Three from Vortex Eight. Four from Vortex Five." "Did you ever see such mangled limbs?"

"Some kind of rock fall in their quarry."

"Liver malfunction... myopia, left eye..."

Others helped unload the grain in which Zed had hidden. This they took into the bakery.

They all spoke with familiarity and joked as they worked, but they were getting dangerously close to his hiding place.

CHAPTER FOUR

The People

Zed ran lightly, through lush greenery, over unfamiliar plants, until he felt it safe to stop. The trees were green with leaf, rich with blossom. Ahead through the branches he saw a larger house. Built of old, carved, and yellowed stone, it still had an added strangeness. Tall transparent domes clustered to form a huge roof above the older structure. Zed watched and wondered, the unfamiliarity of habitations in good order being new to him. How unlike the smoke-blackened gaping windows were those in front of him. Glass glistened in every pane. How unlike the smashed tiles and rafters was the magical roof on the house before him. So far from the ruined cities of the Outlands. Everything was in exquisite order, even the plants underfoot seemed constructed and neatly painted.

He picked one and held it to the ring. "What is it?"

"Flower."

"For what?"

"Decorative."

The object, so neat and richly colored, fell from his fingers.

There was a sound, high and hypnotic, that grew from the trees. A girl had appeared, like magic from the woods, bare-breasted, blonde, astride a white horse. She gazed at him, through him, her eyes penetrating his deepest places. She was one of the other people, yet she had not the disdain in her face, only infinite love and knowledge.

Zed checked his crystal ring – was this one of its hallucinations?

Then there were others, suddenly visible as their combined song rose. They sat in groups within the high branches and at the foot of one great tree, a giant cyprus. They were apart from him, in some other world that he could not see, joined by their song, their meditation.

Was the beautiful girl inviting him to join with them, to become one with their music? It could be no trap, Zed felt, yet it seemed to offer a new and infinite universe for him as he went forward, drawn toward it.

She waited on her horse, passive and all-knowing. She was no illusion but more beautiful than any of his vivid sleep-visions, where such godlike women often walked.

Then she was gone, the spell broken. Leaves fluttered in another direction. The carriers of the maimed ones approached; Zed followed them closely, but still kept under cover. It brought him nearer to the house. The smooth green grass rolled out in front of him. In the center of the lawn stood a pyramid, as tall as he, made of a hard, bright, smooth substance that almost rang with reflected light. Those carrying the bodies walked behind the pyramid, and did not reappear, the long line somehow eaten up by this small structure.

Zed leaned back against a tree, gazed at the ring, the pyramid, the house. He breathed deep, and then moved quickly, running down through the woods, to something which he knew and needed – clear water.

Zed drank deep. The cold surface reassured him. It reflected the clouds and the dark lands beyond that he knew well. The icy liquid refreshed him, clearing his thoughts. This was all real. At the lakeside Zed regained himself.

Someone approached silently along the water's edge. A

woman, moving on foot, evenly, directly at him, for him. He turned and swung toward her, gun aiming. He felt it was too late, although she was nearly naked, and unarmed, alone upon the beach. He was afraid.

Sharp blinding pain leaped from her eyes and into his. He staggered out into the shallows, the gun flying from him, whether thrown from his hand or drawn from it he could not tell, except that she was the source of his agony.

Disarmed, he faced her. She had a beauty like the other woman, yet it was stronger – there was a threat here. Her auburn hair flowed around her face, the eyes were slightly slanted and, like the corners of her mouth, they held a mocking certainty, a power and grace. She was an adversary.

"Do you know where you are?"

"A Vortex..."

"You come from the Outlands. You were told about the Vortex?"

"Zardoz says..." He looked about him nervously, the pain she had given him was real, he felt defenseless. What was her plan? Could she see into his mind, determine truth from falsehood? He must have time.

"What does Zardoz say?" Her eyes bored into his. He rose up.

"Zardoz says that if you obey him you'll go to a Vortex when you die and there you'll live forever..."

"Happily?"

"Yes."

"So you think you're dead?"

"Am I?"

He looked out over the silent dreaming lake. He who knew death so well was yet a stranger to it. Could this be the place beyond death?

He was still sweating but he felt more confident. He must avoid those painful eyes. She moved toward him. His back was to the lake, he could not run.

"You're an Exterminator?" Another question-statement for him.

"I kill for Zardoz." He could back away no farther, yet still she advanced.

"You came here in the stone head."

"I don't know."

"It's the only path and passage into the Vortex. You will show me how you come to be here."

It was quiet. Light from the setting sun played on the water. A shaft of sunlight made a Jacob's ladder between them. Her face was averted as she stood, deep in thought.

He was able to appraise her as a woman for the first time as the sun illuminated the line of her full breast, her narrow hip. Then she turned to face him. Conscious now of the change in him, she was unsettled. He felt more sure of himself, a feeling to be short-lived.

"You have a name."

"Zed."

"Zed," she echoed.

The sunlight caught her left breast and seemed to separate it from her body. Zed was entranced with its beauty, paralyzed by its power. His eyes were drawn upward to hers, fearfully dragged there. A silent bolt of light flashed again from her eyes into his brain, worse than the first shock when he had lost his gun. This one drilled deeper than any bullet, yet he lived... but fell into the darkness and the void beneath his feet, skewered on the pin of light.

CHAPTER FIVE

Subterranean Interrogation

Zed was at home again, hunting.

They galloped along by the sea's edge, sometimes splashing through the breaking foam, always scudding after the prey.

Spurts of sand kicked up by their horses' hooves were echoed by the bullets plowing into the ground, the occasional shot that had gone wide.

It was more fun to use the lance, to spike the prey. Some preferred to cut with the saber. To Zed all three means were as one.

They scampered ahead, some falling, others turning off to try to draw the hunters away, the females trying to protect their young.

The tenacity with which these lower beings clung to life was great, and gave spice to the hunt.

Zed leaned forward and stuck the bobbing man in the back. The little figure stopped pacing his horse's head and vanished from view. Another target. This man still carried the lance that had split his back, there was life in him still. Zed passed him up: live prey was best. He swung down and executed a perfect cut. The head flew from the shoulders of the Brutal below him.

He rose in his stirrups and cut down on the other side, severing another creature from his breath by hacking clean through from neck to hip. Zed's men roared approval. It was a good day.

"I love one that puts up a good fight. I love to see them running. I love the moment of their death when I am One with Zardoz." Zed heard his own voice speaking these words.

"Its coordination is exceptional." Another voice came in to cloud Zed's brain. Was this voice a dream from the past, or future? Was this life he could feel and breathe itself a dream? The voice had a ring of memory: of an auburn-haired girl, by a lake.

Zed galloped past the main body of dead and dying, leaving them to his followers. He had his eyes on better game. The woman was fleet of foot. Like the others she was dirty, dressed in tatters, and she splashed along the sea edge.

Unlike the other females, she had not tried to offer herself, or to protect her young. She must be fresh and untried. A good specimen.

Zed leaned back in his saddle and drew his net. He cast it high and wide ahead of her. It snaked out, then spread, fanlike, around her. As it snapped shut at her thrashing limbs, Zed reined in, leaped from his horse, and was on her. He kissed her lip, then bit into it as she struggled less and less.

The dream returned to him. The auburn-haired woman who had hurt him had a friend, another woman like herself, proud and strong. She had pale eyes, brown hair, was dressed in green clothing. Taller than the first, she had an icy gaze and deep disdain of him. The two conferred, within a glacial, smooth windowless chamber, glancing down at him from time to time. He was pinioned, or so it seemed. The dream swam away.

He mounted the captured woman. He spent himself and

rose, dragging her after him. She was fine booty, to be taken home across his saddle, to bear a child for Zardoz's sake.

The image ran out of his mind and left blankness.

Zed cleared. The two women looked down at him. They had faces filled with disgust. It was as if the last scene had reversed itself. Zed was the weakling, trapped in an invisible net. The women were his captors, his future leaders and owners. He felt as the Brutals had felt, but he was still strong beneath it all. Although Zardoz had betrayed him, although he was captured deep within the Vortex by two women the like of which amazed him, he was alive.

His mind was being stretched back to that day beside the sea. The memory was drawn out of him by the two women.

"Zarday 312 – twenty-five Brutals exterminated. Took a woman in his name – Zardoz."

He rose up from the girl and gazed out at the sea and sand. He had no word for "beach."

"A place where the sea meets the land."

He wrenched his mind to perceive the reality of the moment. The two women were draining his mind and projecting it onto a wall. He was their mental puppet, a plaything to be rewound and looked at in their own time. He struggled up through layers of their strength. The memory would stop.

The brown-haired one spoke.

"It's blacked again, May. It seems to be able to control its memory."

The other ignored her and commanded Zed.

"Show us more of your work."

Zed felt his mind slipping again, back and back.

It was a wheat field. It was a sunny day. Twenty Brutals

were working, rhythmically forward, to the sound of the drum. Zed's mind could also see the room in which he lay, as well as relive those moments in that field.

The walls tapered upward. They were glassy black. Above him opened a slim black shaft set in the ceiling; it vanished into darkness. The walls seemed to pulse. Behind their glassy exterior was life, wet, fresh, and frightful. Yet on one wall was *his* life.

The two women, May and the other, were in some way drawing his thoughts from him as he lay on a slab in the center of the room. They were making them appear, as bright as his day had been. They talked into the rings they wore. That would be the machinery of his predicament. The crystal ring again, always at the center.

One of the Brutals stumbled. Zed raised his arm and fired. Shot him dead straight through his head. The man fell. The others continued digging. It was during the time of growing and planting. May spoke. "When is this, Consuella?"

"This is a more recent memory, cultivation has started."

"Zardoz made us grow crops," cried Zed.

The pressure on Zed's mind lessened. The weights withdrew somewhat. The two women conferred, their wispy, fragile clothing contradicting their tough intent.

"Disturbed?" asked May.

"A little." Consuella was more concerned than she would admit.

"The Outlands have to be controlled." May might be somehow in his favor. Could she be an ally at a future date? Zed had surfaced into an argument about himself.

"I have always voted against forced farming"

"You eat the bread." May again, sarcastic.

"We have to shut ourselves off – we have to – "

May came back – to his aid?

"This is the first visual contact with the Outlands in years – as opposed to data – since Arthur was delegated to control them. It's proper that we investigate."

"It's better not to know, these images will pollute us... Quench it! Quell it!"

Zed allowed himself to flash his eyes to the left, to gaze into the black depths of the wall. Within, there swam figures, naked mutilated bodies. Consigned there from the head perhaps. One body lacked a leg; around the stump a membrane protected what could have been a new limb, growing. Smaller and more hideous figures floated deep behind the first. He was buried in a liquid vault, trapped in a pocket of air, numbed and paralyzed while two icy beings discussed his life and death.

Zed followed the women with his eyes. May stood still gazing at the screen. Consuella padded up to her and took her in her arms, stroked her hair, kissed her, imploringly. May was cold, the images still fascinated her.

"Perhaps it can tell us how Arthur has vanished so mysteriously."

"May, please." Consuella put her hand on May's shoulder, but May was moving to the screen.

"Is Arthur Frayn's memory transmission still functioning?"

The familiar voice of the ring answered, smooth and calm. "Arthur Frayn ceased transmission three days ago."

"Replay his last memory moments."

Zed had nowhere to run, even if he could have moved his legs. Terror filled him.

On the screen came the swirling fall of Arthur Frayn, the clouds, the rain exactly as it was before and yet distorted through a memory, as Zed's had been. An elaborate reconstruction of reality; true to yet larger than eye's vision.

The ground rushed up and engulfed the viewers... blackness.

"Play back the preceding images so we can discover how he suffered this fall."

The images on the screen went into reverse.

"It is permitted only to show the accident. No other memory-image may be played without the consent of the individuals concerned."

The scene stopped, then rolled forward again.

"Arthur Frayn... died. Reconstruction has begun."

May and Consuella moved over to examine the interior of one wall section. They illuminated a tiny fetus, growing behind the glass. Zed felt a chill of horror. May spoke, almost endearingly. "Ah yes. There." Consuella swung around in anger, certain now that Zed should die.

"That's an end to it! Kill it, May!"

"No."

"May, for our love."

"Consuella!"

"Don't!" They struggled, one trying to embrace the other. May held Consuella off. "I will invoke a community vote."

Consuella responded, "The community will follow my intuition."

"Then I'll go to the Vortex," May was adamant, Consuella anguished. "You're hurting me!"

May was bending over Zed now. "This is an experiment, Consuella. We must find out how it came here. Where is Arthur Frayn? How did you come into the stone?"

Zed felt her eyes again and a veil rose over his mind. He

could just feel the image of Zardoz, flying. The picture was displayed on the screen unerringly.

"Zardoz... the stone..." The veil was drawn.

Once again Zed was hunting, unwillingly replaying his life. They rode out proudly, wearing the masks of Zardoz.

Carefully fashioned in the likeness of their God, the huge helmets had faces front and back, to horrify the Brutals and to praise their King. The Brutals broke in fear and ran from their swords, no terror masks were necessary. The Brutals scattered over the dunes in fright as the riders bore down on them.

"Those ridiculous masks."

"But it's so beautiful."

Zed felt a new surrounding. He was standing paralyzed but for his past and a tiny section of his mind that could see out – into a large orange room, a new location.

Now there were others around him. The two women and others like them. The men were strangely like the women, effete, gilded, decorative. He felt them to be more passive than the females. They all crowded around the screen, laughing and applauding. This was the community, perhaps twenty-five in all. This was what he had come to see. He had penetrated the heart of a Vortex.

They were exotically caparisoned, men and women wearing variations of a single style. Head scarves revealed their faces but fanned out to cover their necks like spreading fans. Tight jackets, open at the throat and tied with bindings across their breasts, flowed out to winglike shoulders. They were girded with jeweled codpieces, heavily woven with metals and belts that secured the wide, divided skirts which stopped at the knee.

Brightly shining buckled shoes completed their costumes.

All were richly jeweled, but in particular each wore a large crystal ring on the third finger of the left hand. This glowed with an inner life of its own.

The materials of their costume varied, some were as fine as butterfly wings, others gaudy, or lustrous with dark velvet and purple silk. It all spoke of much wealth in time, ingenuity, and construction.

Their tight bodices revealed lithe bodies rippling beneath the thongings. Slim-hipped and long-limbed, their dress showed them as beautiful and young, displaying their bodies for all love's eyes and promises.

In addition some carried, toga-like, a length of the finest, most carefully patterned cloth thrown around them. Like colored smoke, it gave their bodies a blurred hue where it touched. Others wore this around them like long cloaks, while some sat inside of them, tent-like, and as the color washed their forms with soft light, so they seemed in tune with other worlds softer and more gentle than the harsh one Zed knew – cocooned, insulated, remote yet visible in their reverie.

His mind was pushed back into the past, his consciousness sank again. It was the beach. He chased along in front of the others. The women

Brutals tried to dissuade him from attack – they offered themselves, all three of them, inviting, enticing.

Zed could not resist. He leaped from his horse.

"My father was chosen... my mother was chosen... only we could breed... only the chosen..."

May's voice cut across his memory. "Selective breeding, do you think? What has Arthur been doing out there all these years?"

Consuella answered: "He never discussed this in the

Vortex. He will have to be thoroughly investigated. This is highly punishable behavior."

"No one else wanted to run the Outlands... He's an artist. He does it with imagination. Allow him that at least."

The voice came from a languid man near Zed. Unlike the others, there seemed to burn another light within; cynicism, doubt perhaps.

The man was of middling height and looks. Strangely nondescript, yet familiar in face and form, a man with whom Zed had ridden, who he'd fought against, and killed, a hundred score of times. A common man, yet spiked with the strong dye of the uncommon. His eyes drooped down like the corners of his mouth so that he looked morosely out upon the world at all times. Then the corners would twitch up quickly as his heart betrayed his mind. A man at once dangerous but resigned, highly intelligent but weak-willed. A second string to another's bow. Zed sensed a cunning, something more devious than those who seemed to best him. His fawning and despair conceded a darker, stronger heart than most.

He looked boyish, almost too thin, his curling hair a trifle too effeminate for his bitter words. Double-edged and mean, his face flickered with warmth and wit, a humor he could not conceal from Zed's sense-vision. A thinker, not a doer; a plotter, shifty, cunning, lean. He was a fox among wolves, but an old gray fox among young she-wolves, a male in a matriarchy. Zed saw that he so loved to be cutting that one day the edge would take off more than his tongue.

Consuella spoke.

"He is potentially renegade, as you well know, Friend."

They are discussing Arthur Frayn again, thought Zed. Then more visions were pulled from him. He must fight to stop them leaving him. He must struggle not to betray himself.

He galloped over the dunes, once more at the head of his column. How good to feel the spray, the sun, the speed of his horse.

The watchers' voices languidly floated in and over his reverie.

"It's terribly exciting."

"But the suffering."

"Oh, you can't equate their feelings with ours."

"It's just entertainment."

Other voices drifted in.

"Where did the Brutals get those clothes?"

"They probably found them in some old whorehouse."

Another sneering remark floated up across the first.

"They *are* very skillful."

"Well, they are inspired with a religious fervor."

Zed felt rather than heard the words, they imported too much meaning for him. Could his life be part of some larger purpose? Was he just an arm of some greater being following its own secret path? He could not comprehend the possible meanings at this time, for his mind was driven back again to reveal the past when he scourged the Earth of the Brutal horde.

Still the other voices floated in, remote but telling.

"It's an absurd proposition."

"There's no precedent for this kind of intrusion."

"Surely we have to investigate possibilities."

They spoke as if he were a mere cipher, a pattern of lines to be erased and reorganized at a planner's whim, but he was a man.

Zed pulled his mind from the past and pushed it up into the present. The screen grew dim and faded. The watchers groaned. Zed was fully conscious now. Friend was at his side, looking at him like a prospective buyer at a slave market.

"Obscenely decaying flesh. The sweet scent of putrefaction already in the air. But it's a fine strong beast, dear May. What exactly do you want to do with it?"

May replied, addressing the community, pleading a case.

"A full genetic study. Break its DNA code, see if there are any structural or evolutional changes since ours were analyzed two hundred years ago. Discover any new hereditary disease factors which may have emerged, that might result in broadening our immunization spectrum. Study its emotional and psychic elements in relation to its sociology."

The audience had gradually followed Friend's lead and were all around Zed now, poking, smoothing, and prodding him. He watched and waited. They were unlike him, though human. All had a curious, ageless look, yet none could have been over twenty; they were children in their movements and manner, yet their eyes were old.

Friend was older than the rest, just a few lines on his face to betray age, work, or worry; nothing more. Except for Zed, no one in the room bore any marks of time; no wounds, no gray hairs, no sagging wrinkles marred their beautiful young bodies. Their minds were different. May and Consuella chaffed a long forgotten friendship that had been much more, social cuts and bruises barely on display, peeping under the trim clothing of community. Friend certainly showed a visible mental wound. He was more alert than the rest but lacked their languid, all-knowing poise. He seemed a man like Zed; someone who was other than he looked, a man with secret knowledge, a heresy that could lead to his destruction, but a secret that could spell the end for others.

Consuella answered May's speech as if it had been a personal attack, but stilled herself and calmly addressed all present.

"That all sounds respectably scientific, but what is May's

underthought? Not long ago she was asking for new births, although we have no deaths. We are perfectly stabilized. We said no to May. Now she wants to bring in this dangerous animal from outside. Think of our equilibrium. Remember the delicate balance we must maintain. Just the presence will disturb our tranquillity. May is a great scientist, but she has destructive tendencies."

The crowd was pressing closer around their captive, fondling, squeezing, touching him. He felt hot, confused, annoyed, but held himself in control. The women were the most interested. He seemed to awake long-forgotten memories in them; as they in him. May and Consuella continued to argue, oblivious of the crowd which now had only eyes, and hands, for him.

"We have adequate means of controlling it, surely we're not so vulnerable..."

Consuella's anger burst across May's voice.

"Look at it! It knows its life is at stake, otherwise it would rape and kill as it always has."

The Eternals glanced at one another in a mounting flurry of confused and differing responses to the seemingly simple man before them. They laughed, argued, but were divided and unsettled. Zed felt he had stayed the hand of execution yet again. If he could continue to divide them against themselves, if he could be a source of disruption to their unity, he would live longer. The flutter of excitement and dissension could be the beginning of a schism that might rend the heart of Vortex Four. He did not allow himself to show pleasure in their discontent, for this would betray that he was more than he seemed, and he had still to keep the face of ignorance. The babble of argument rose around him. Zed maintained his air of innocence.

Consuella's voice was lost. "See the disrupting effect..."

Friend chimed in. "Let's keep it, anything to relieve the boredom."

Arguing broke out. They began to squabble like children over a new toy.

Consuella's face calmed as she turned to another figure who had been watching, still and silent in the shadows. Zed followed her gaze. It was the girl he had first seen upon the white horse. The girl who had looked into his heart, who knew him to the core, and yet had not betrayed him then. Would she now?

The room became still, the attention fell away from Zed as the girl flowed silently across the room. The giant screen was now blank, and columns of bright gauze seemed to hang in midair, not unlike the vehicles for transporting the bodies which Zed had seen within the Zardoz head. Yet these were fine-woven tubelike shapes that seemed to lack a living center. They moved gossamer-like as she passed, as if in obeisance to her. She was regal but not haughty; very young but wise as time.

Consuella greeted her.

"This is a psychic disturbance. Avalow – what does it portend for the future?"

She gazed at Zed, and once again he felt unafraid and calm. She looked into him. She could see all of him, the man he had been, the present Zed, and perhaps the one to come. He knew now that she would never reveal him to the others. He saw trust and compassion in her face, emotions he had never known before, and as he looked, she changed.

Avalow became translucent, seemed to glow. She spoke. "How did we conjure up a monster in our midst, and why? This is the question we must answer."

As she finished speaking she gradually reverted to a substantial girl, mortal, beautiful, and real.

There was a pause as the group digested what she had said. Witchlike, she smiled and moved away. Talking started; small knots of people became earnestly locked into private discussions, using a brief, weird vocal compression that Zed could not understand. Except that he was at its center. Should he run now, while they were in debate, while there was still time?

Before he could move he felt a gentle pressure on his arm. It was Friend, smiling Friend.

"Well, you've set the fur flying, my beauty. I wonder what's going on in your pea-brain, eh?"

He ruffled Zed's hair, as he might a dog's fur.

"I like you, you sly old monster, do you hear?" Cast as a dog, Zed licked the hand that patted him. Friend recoiled.

Each seemed to understand the other. Man and servant, but brothers in a future crime.

The patter was quickening behind them; the strange words and signs flowed back and forth, gathering into a common voice.

"Vote, vote, vote!"

A woman spoke up from the throng. "In favor?"

Zed watched, intrigued, as they began to signal to her a complex series of patterns, not just yea or nay, but other details passing between the teller and the voters.

"Against."

Her eyes passed over them, calculating, correlating.

Zed felt uneasy, although the performance was intriguing. May flashed a triumphant glance at Consuella, who looked back angrily. May walked proudly as if in victory. She signaled to Zed to follow her, which he did.

As they left, Friend whispered in Zed's ear. "Congratulations. A stay of execution. Three weeks!"

CHAPTER SIX

The Beginning of the End

Friend shoved him through the iron doorway of a cage and clanged it shut. Zed surveyed them and the scene beyond. Friend stood with a man Zed would come to know as George Saden, another victim of the system. They both presented their inscrutable Eternal faces to him.

"You'll be working for me tomorrow, Monster. My other horse died last week."

They turned and walked off past the other cages of curious animals, leaving Zed to contemplate the tumultuous events of his first day in the Vortex.

This antique farmyard was refitted as an animal prison. Male and female of all species that were hardy and of man's Earth were here, his cattle and his beasts of burden; and tucked away into one tight corner, near a giant gateway that swallowed up all light, the smallest section of all, the hominids: lip-service homage to the Eternals' ancestors, monkeys, an ape or two, and now, the prize relation, Zed.

At least he was almost out of doors. He would be able to see the moon and breathe fresh night air through the bars of his cage. The straw was clean, as was the pitcher full of water; some grain mash lay there too. And there were three whole weeks before they killed him.

* * *

"Well, Monster. Up and time for work."

The cage clanged open in the morning sun. Zed shuffled ahead of Friend, out of the courtyard and through the stone archway. Consuella and some others were feeding and grooming the animals. Zed was surprised to see them doing menial tasks – slave-work. As they crossed into the dark gate, Friend caught Zed's back a blow with a whip, knocking him forward into the walls of the exit corridor. Zed spun back ready to strike but was quickly bit with a deadly look from Friend's eyes. Not as strong as the one from May that had rendered him unconscious, but painful just the same.

"All right. Let's stop all the nonsense, shall we? Where's Arthur Frayn?"

Zed did not move or speak.

"You ever hear the expression 'if looks could kill'? Well, here they can. There's no need to pretend with me. I am not as the others – I know more than you think – I'm in Arthur Frayn's confidence... Zardoz."

He waited to see the effect of his speech, but Zed kept silent, neither his face nor body betraying a response.

"All right – we'll wait and see..."

They walked toward an old clock tower that stood apart from the rest of the buildings, just as Friend was apart from the Eternals yet of them.

"Don't be sullen – I'm going to look after you. Whenever you're ready, ask me questions – anything you like."

Friend passed his crystal ring across the doorway in a certain pattern. It swung back to show a long flight of stone steps running into the earth below. With a charming smile and a slight bow, Friend invited Zed to lead the way down.

"This is where you'll be working each morning. Just menial tasks, nothing too taxing."

Friend always concealed a second meaning in his taunting words. Was Friend offering himself as an ally?

The steps seemed almost as endless as the shaft into the pyramid. The air became cooler. They would soon be on a level with the interrogation room and its adjoining columns of darkness and mystery.

Zed turned to Friend. "Is this your God's house?"

"Ah – it's gods you're seeking, is it?" He laughed. They had reached the bottom of the staircase.

The corridor opened out into a huge vaulted arena, its ceiling lost high in darkness. It was crammed with statues in countless poses, from every culture. They stood frozen, peering out at each other over partly emptied wooden crates that spilled smaller objects onto the floor. The huge area was stuffed with the museum art of centuries, the aspirations, the dreams, the art of a dozen civilizations.

"Here you are. Gods, goddesses, kings, and queens. Take your pick."

They walked along a natural corridor formed from two rows of grotesque statues that walled back an infinity of further idols.

"But they're all dead."

"Dead?" Zed echoed.

"Died of boredom." Friend began to laugh again, a melancholy bitter laugh that rattled off the dead stone around him.

Friend's headquarters met with Zed's approval. He had loosely assembled some favorite objects from the booty around him, pushed in some comfortable chairs, then let things grow around his trackways. They rested at the natural center of this mad maze. Where their paths intersected in the meanderings through the countless treasures was Friend's living area; dusty, bitty, vivid. Piles of books, the first Zed had seen here, cluttered the floor. Even they had been gradually pushed into the surface of a landscape – Friend's home.

Friend strode through it all, talking to Zed the while.

"This is where I work, Monster. I ferret around here looking for clues. It all started hundreds of years ago when I was younger than you see me now, not that it shows, of course. It was simply a scientific process – annotate, tabulate, draw conclusions from the past. But the deeper I burrowed, the more involved I became. I thought that all these treasures from other worlds held the secrets of their endings, but they only reflected the certainty of *our* own fall, while keeping *their* information to themselves. I must admit, I love it. The more I find, the less I know. Just as I get one set of notions organized, another situation disproves them. Everything is dissimilar and delightful, yet all things seem the same. It's not a job, it's a nonstop voyage. Once I was an ascetic academic, now I'm just a cynical treasure-finder. You wouldn't understand that, would you – or is there more to you than just an ugly face?"

He stooped in his travels and picked up a broom which he threw at Zed. "We all must work, Monster, keep at it now. No slacking or you won't go to Heaven."

The master worked at his desk, while the servant Zed swept up in an idle, rhythmic, ineffectual way. But Zed found time to poke a finger through the eye of a painted portrait. Both men were happy in their work.

Friend was using his communicator ring to project pictures on the wall. Wheeled vehicles flashed on and off the screen, starting with cart-like carriages that Zed could see might have been useful if pulled by a horse. They flashed through many changes, the vehicles gradually growing smoother and glossier, sleeker and more metallic. Friend was angry with the pictures. He shouted into his ring. "That's wrong!"

"It is catalogued according to your instructions."

"I wanted you to analyze design growth across all makes of car – not just a chronological list from one manufacturer!"

"A much more complex program. Shall I seek Vortex consent for a longer program?" Dully the voice repeated its statement until Friend angrily barked "Yes!" to quiet it.

"It will take time," the voice continued. "There is a stack-up on some circuits."

Zed was enjoying the argument. Man against magic ring. Friend's beady eye swiveled and caught him smiling.

"Well, I've got time, plenty of it. Define three weeks!"

Zed started at this. It was a comment suddenly too close to his heart.

"Twenty-one days – 504 hours – 30,240 minutes – 1,814,400 seconds."

As the figures defining Zed's lifetime rattled forward, he picked up a clock that stood on a shelf and moved its hands back. A sudden whir preceded a clash of chimes that made Zed start and Friend laugh.

Friend leaned back, enjoying Zed's discomfort. Should Zed trust this malicious creature? Could he confide in him? Zed sensed danger in that course. Something held him back.

Zed was once again May's property. She led him through a tunnel and out into another, calmer room. They left the contemplation space where the cocoons rose to the ceiling and formed the high transparent dome Zed had seen the first time the house had come into his view. He connected the glittering bulges in the sunshine high above the building which surrounded it, and in which it was centered, with the room behind him.

They padded through the darkened way and entered the dining room.

A huge mirrored table was set for all the community. Simple foods and eating utensils were laid out around its edge. A huge vine grew up and over the table so that grapes hung from its lowering branches. The room was large and old, and had the look of an area that had been traditionally a place of gathering and good cheer for generations. It had nothing of the mystic and ascetic look of the room they had just left.

A gentle sound of tiny bells filled the air as they swung in the light breeze wafting in the windows, sounding like the chimes that had so chilled Zed in Friend's museum. Friend and a colleague chuckled as they saw Zed and May approach.

"You mean to say he never saw a clock before?"

Friend laughingly replied, "Obviously not."

Consuella saw the couple, too, and asked, "Are you not taking food with us, May?"

Some others joined in the gentle derision, tittering and smirking.

"She is taking her studies seriously."

"Well – she only has three weeks."

May, like Zed, was unmoved in her path, and took his hand and led him on.

They went past another doorway, where skeins of transparent cloth made a rainbow film between the far window and the door. A place of weaving.

May led him to the vaulted window across the black polished floor, then out into the green garden beyond, toward the shiny pyramid that sat among the statuary and the flowers.

Consuella watched them go. She and the others had followed through the dark avenue to the room of eating.

The group filed in and took up their accustomed places around the table.

Consuella, too, was in hers now.

She watched the retreating couple with a glance that betrayed envy.

Raising her crystal ring, she softly spoke into it.

"Do you know yet how the Brutal came here?"

"No conclusion; insufficient data received."

They passed a loaf of bread from hand to hand, each kissing it in turn, in homage to the fruits of the field.

A ritual blessing and thanksgiving.

It was as if the Brutal had never been among them.

The prayer over, they fell to eating, chattering and laughing.

At the pyramid side, May beckoned to Zed. He approached warily.

"Go in."

She moved her hand across the hard mirror surface, using the ring to point at certain places. The glassy surface parted as if it had been water. The flat surface changed to a dark shaft, vanishing into a void below his feet. There were traces of hard walls all around; no steps or handrail, just the pit.

"Go in."

He felt a hard push and was falling down and down, into the center of the pyramid. He had entered at the tip, the only point which showed above the ground, and was falling faster and faster, with nothing to stop him. As he tumbled he caught a glimpse of May falling after him, straight and slim.

The tube yawned open and distended outward around him. He was falling into the interrogation room; the room where Frayn was regrowing, straight as the slab on which he had lain before.

Zed's arms flailed as he tried to stop his fall. He heard a low laugh, then May and he floated to a soft stop on the hard floor. She landed like a leaf on water, he like a pole-axed ox.

The pyramid's only gateway was the most cunning entrance through which he had ever passed. It knew all who came through, checking them first. The ring was a key and an identifying ornament. The sheer shaft meant the pyramid had absolute power over those entering. If it felt like killing, it could let those falling speed on to their certain deaths.

How did the damaged bodies get behind the glass? Perhaps the slab on which Frayn lay opened downward as a means of entry and exit; doubtless just as cleverly constructed and guarded. The pyramid, or whatever ruled here, was an impregnable fortress, doubly locked in all its cunning doorways.

Zed continued to reflect on this new enclosure. He must have been unconscious the first time he made his entrance down the shaft, still stunned by May's look. She must have carried him, yet she looked so frail. The powers of these people seemed endless.

The other point on which he pondered was how he had left this place before. The buffering device which had let them down so gently must be employed in reverse to lift them slowly up the shaft to the top when the analysis was over. Again it showed how well-planned this place had been. He was powerless against it; one could be trapped forever down here, with those grim fetal creatures behind the glass. Arthur Frayn was regrowing fast right next to him.

Now May was bending low over Zed, using the ring as a viewing device. She looked at him as if he were a specimen from the,fields; a lowly creature, but one of more than passing interest. May could see things within him that he had not suspected.

"Keep still. Look into the ring."

As he gazed into the thin flat front of the ring, he felt it scan his inner eye, and after a moment saw patterns of veins displayed on the screen in front of him. May froze them, or perhaps the ring kept the image still. Then she observed this plan in silence. Zed felt there were other rooms, other vaults within the pyramid. Could they contain the machinery of the ring? How could one gain access to it? Were there duplicates in other caves ready to take this one's place should it be damaged? He felt there would be brother organisms, far from this place, ready, silent, and waiting. A worthy foe, a matchless army.

And yet if one could get to the soul of an enemy, it could be destroyed, even though it was almighty.

If the spirit was broken, the body would fall.

The bright latticework of blood vessels moved into life again, each one a living line of life.

"No retinal abnormalities. The fundus is normal. Disk and retinal vessels are normal. There are no hemorrhages or exudates. Macula area is clear."

It was the familiar voice that had so frightened Zed in the cottage. It sounded too indifferent to be a leader, yet more confident than a slave. Did the owner of the voice live underground; nearby?

The picture came closer, one vein grew before Zed's eyes.

May watched it impassively, then she muttered to the ring again and the picture jumped even closer, the blood cells themselves filling the screen. She froze the picture, spoke again as if noting a detail, and was again lost in the mechanics of discovery.

The flat voice of the ring cut across her contemplation.

"Continuation of the trial of George Saden of Vortex Four."

May angrily watched her chosen picture fade in favor of a blank face: a man, one of the group.

"George Saden, accused of transmitting a negative aura in the second level."

The man began to speak. May watched intently, but tapped her foot as if to hurry him along.

"This is not so. I have studied our social emotional substructures for one hundred forty years. My thoughts are constructive criticisms, pyramidical. I am innocent of psychic violence. As you examine my face and eyes you will see this is true."

Zed could imagine the fluttering voting hands, the garbled voices chattering back their comments to the main voice. The man's face before him twitched slightly, then shook as it realized its error. The muscles had betrayed the man. Zed liked him.

"He's lying," murmured May.

Zed had come full circle. Again he stood in the courtyard by the bakery, this time a beast of burden and not a hunter. He waited between the shafts of a little cart while Friend loaded it to the brim with the green loaves. Others bustled around, in and out of the bakery. Zed gazed out of the main gate, remembering how the head had landed there, bringing him into this place, just a few days before. Friend saw his look.

"Looking for the head, Monster? It's gone. Off on its endless journey, from Vortex to Vortex around and around – like me with the bread – forever and ever."

A scuffle among the workers broke into Friend's musings. It seemed that one of the men had hurt a woman with his eyes, just as Zed had been stung, though not quite so sharply. But it was the first aggressive move Zed had seen among them. Other Eternals surged forward to pull away the man who had committed physic violence. Friend got on board and jogged Zed forward like the horse he was.

"Will he be punished for that?"

"Of course," said Friend knowingly, smiling with memories.

They moved through wooded lanes away from the main buildings and down toward the lake where Zed had first encountered May.

"But you have no police, no Exterminators."

Friend laughed. "Oh, we discuss it endlessly. Every little sin and misdemeanor. Raked over and over – "

"Then what happens to him?"

"He'll get six months for that at least."

"Prison?"

Friend laughed. "No. Aging."

Aging, what could he mean by it?

"I'm getting old myself," Friend said languidly from his comfortable seat on the cart. "Six months here. A year there. These sentences add up. They age you, but they don't let you die."

"Why not kill yourself?" Zed ventured.

"I do now and again, but the Eternal Tabernacle simply rebuilds me." Another sardonic thought struck him, twisting a smile onto his lips.

"Do you want to see immortality at work?" said Friend to the panting Zed, and so saying gave him a jog down a new road and up a hill. A curious building came in sight. Letters spiked above a low one-story building: STARLIGHT HOTEL. The words had outgrown what they described, a flower dwarfing its roots, belying them. The bizarre decoration promised a much grander platform than the one from which it came.

Friend chuckled at Zed's confusion. "This is where they live – the Renegades. They are condemned to an eternity of senility. We provide them with food, but they are shunned. They are malicious and vicious, so in and out fast. I, myself, feel quite at home in there."

They rattled toward a huge glass doorway that stood open. Some thirty old people reached out to meet them. They were ancients. The room was decayed and frightful. Tatters of decorations hung down like creepers from the ceiling. A three-piece band tootled from a tiny stand at one end of the hall. The ancients wore evening dress, yellowed, patched, frayed, and torn. Around the floor, in what had been dining booths, others, too old to move, lay in cribs.

Zed sped in to the dance floor, drawing the cart fast, then skidded in a turn to take them straight out again as Friend hurled out the loaves. The ancients were galvanized and ran shrieking to the food. They fought and clawed for the bread, reducing it to scraps and crumbs as the cart burst into the sunshine once again and off down the path back into the woods. The cackles of the Renegades followed them down the gentle hill.

They clattered into a new place. High gates were open. Another courtyard was before them, formed of bleak cottages. As they rolled by, Friend threw loaves of bread into doorways. No faces appeared, it was a dead place.

He steered the cart into a barn that opened from the yard, then jumped down. Zed, relieved of the burden, stepped from the shafts, lowering the cart.

Winded, Zed stepped back – onto something.

The room was filled with people. They had the mien of the transported ones, except they weren't contained in cloth cocoons. They had the familiar look of Friend's statues. They were certainly alive, but what kind of life was it?

Friend smiled at Zed's bewilderment. He pointed to a dead-faced girl. "I loved this girl once, Monster." Then, to the crowded room, "You idle Apathetics are a melancholy sight."

The soft gong sound came from his ring, interrupting him.

"You are asked to vote at the termination of the trial of George Saden. Final statement from the accused begins."

George Saden was projected onto Friend's face through the ring. The inhabitants turned their heads slowly to look at him.

Saden began to speak, and as he did so, the others gathered in frightful slow motion around them, forming a fence of deathly people.

"I confess to the charges. I try to suppress these thoughts, but they leak out in second level through the head wound of my third death. I was imperfectly repaired." His face changed, becoming defiant. "No – it is not true! I think what I think!"

Friend smiled down at him. "That's more like it! I'm with you, George."

It was as if George heard him.

"I hate you all, I hate you all, I hate you all – especially me."

The image faded.

"Vote please. Vote please."

The people around them seemed aware but powerless

to act. Either from atrophy or months of idle sub-emotions, their bodies stood – on the edge of life and reason.

Friend talked into the ring.

"I'm voting for the poor sod. It won't do any good, nothing does... Absolute acquittal."

Zed walked up to one exquisitely beautiful girl who seemed to be looking at him. He grasped a breast, then squeezed it. No response. She was still slowly focusing back from where he had been to where he was now, her nervous system, minutes behind his, dulled and defeated.

Friend smirked. "Go on – help yourself!"

Zed caressed the girl, gently, then fiercely. She submitted blindly with no response to him – for or against. Friend walked among the others and placed their arms in weird positions. There they stayed, then slowly sank back to their original positions, through the liquid air.

"Didn't Zardoz tell you about the Apathetics? No? It's a disease and it's slowly creeping all through the Vortexes. That's why Zardoz made you grow crops – to feed these people. We can't support them anymore. Apathetic or Renegade – take your choice."

Zed gulped at the information and it stuck inside him. His God was a grain-ship to feed these infirm people. Emotional mutes, sad statues that were once Eternals. Zed saw them clearly, he saw inside them, and there lay a voice. This could consume him. He felt the pull of their great sad emptiness and was afraid. No enemy had been so passive yet so strong. Their very weakness was their strength. He felt them pulling him like the spirits of the dead into a grave that had no end. These Apathetics drew him to an endless night, where he could see and feel but not move. To be paralyzed by some great insect demon, like a helpless grub, and then to live on while the canker of another vulture ate into his live but mordant flesh. They had ceased to live and yet they could never die. He felt the process starting, his limbs were leaden. He could not move. The soft assurance of the living dead enfolded him. He felt an awful sleep come upon his face and neck, his eyes dropped and glazed. He could not scream, he was buried alive in the thin crisp air.

His heart still fluttered at its steady speed but slowed a trifle, sinking him to their torpor. His blood was cooling down to their icy level. Then his heart stirred and pumped faster. He would not be drawn into their web. His blood pulsed quicker and his brain began to fight the numbness of their gaze. He would survive and win. He would endure. He would surmount them all. His body sang, his limbs, flexed, he was alive, he sprang.

Zed picked up the girl and threw her into a pile of straw, where she lay like a monstrous doll.

Zed smashed a barrel into the wall. He overturned a cart and roared out his life's energy in a cry. Some of the Apathetics stirred, some rose to their feet. The girl's eyes flickered from the straw, perhaps with fear. Zed stopped, spent. Friend clapped ironically.

"Good – now you're beginning to show yourself."

Zed felt the clammy hand of despair touch him for the first time. The nameless, faceless foe that confronted him seemed overwhelming.

The gong rang again. The Apathetics settled once more into their sea-bed trances.

"Final votes: For: nine; against: five hundred and eighty-six; undecided: eighty-six. George Saden will be aged five years."

Friend scowled, then his face cleared, and he turned to Zed.

"Welcome to Paradise!"

The commune was assembled. Once again Zed was on show in the large orange room.

As they examined him, so he looked back at them.

There were not more than thirty active members at any time. The building and the grounds could accommodate a great many more. Where were they now? Either Apathetic or Renegade.

Time was wasting, drawing him to his execution date. How would they kill him? He knew death, but the Eternals' stoical mixture of superior knowledge, emotional indifference, and perpetual childhood chilled him. They were like the wicked, spoiled children of some giant father who had abandoned them in this luxurious nursery. Perhaps they gradually grew to adulthood over hundreds of years. Had they dispatched their elders? Was he at the mercy of genius infants who had the intellect of gods but were swept by more sinister feelings than he could comprehend?

He calmed as he saw what was happening to his thoughts. It was true that his thinking was beginning to slide toward panic. What did he *know?*

The ring: each member of the commune wore one. With it they could speak to each other and to a central being who could assemble, organize, and relay this and other information back to them. A central being presided over all the Tabernacle. The pyramid: an underground fortress. It might have been built as a shelter against an enemy and a force of which Zed could not conceive. Certainly it was impregnable and contained the core of the community.

They called it the Tabernacle room. To him it was a place of interrogation and horror.

Here it was they were remade if they were damaged or killed. Which led him to the last fact – they were Eternal. His hosts would never die. Even if he eliminated them all they would start to regrow deep underground and reappear miraculously like the spring corn from the ground, the exact match of the last crop. He knew that the womblike machinery worked faster than its human counterpart. Frayn, the man he had shot, the man who had seemed so certain about Zed, would return in a few days, fully formed, with all his faculties and memories intact, to confront him.

So the central mind was hidden, protected by thin air; the only entry to it was through the crystal on the ring. The Tabernacle was impregnable.

The Eternals could never be destroyed.

He was their prisoner, temporarily, until death or escape stepped in. All these facts were real.

And yet there were other meanings, other signs around him that imported other stories with hope for him. The leaders were May and Consuella, once united by more than common interest; by love. This powerful union had long ended. He could feel old hungers stirring in them. Were they for him and for his lust, or was it for revenge on his tough male reality? May seemed the weaker of the two at present, but she had a large group of followers, silent, discreet, all female, all devoted to her. Consuella, though the stronger, was alone. He felt her deadly presence. She could not be bought or flanked. She would be victorious or vanquished.

There was dissension at the center of the group; he could help to take it further.

Friend could be an ally, but was he too remote and weak

like all the men here? He lived on the edge of the tribe, and might soon be cast into exile. Dare Zed follow him as a comrade, or would such effort be misspent? Apathy might soon be fate. At least the existence of those half-dead Apathetics showed the Vortex to be failing. It showed the central plan to be at fault. If it had failed here, Zed could make it fail elsewhere.

Yet all the inmates here were gifted and special. Each had his own sphere of knowledge, but each had to work as a menial every day. Apparently they needed to keep in touch with earth and air, for they were almost nothing more than spirits. Zed was live and strong, his soul was one with his body; these people were near wraiths compared to him. They were always being interrupted to be one with the governing process, while in Zed's tribe all was happily talk or action. Here wrangling and petty conflicts neutered change.

He must keep them guessing; the longer he intrigued them, the longer he would live.

He must continue to divide them, amaze them, the while striving to gain entry to the secret center. His life was slipping by, they would soon kill him. They were without heart as he was, and yet they lacked an inner fire.

They were safe, secure, and wise. He had not seen one predator or giant cat since his arrival. No raiders swooped and killed. No person went armed or had need to, so why their agitation over him? He must soon find where May had put his gun, for armed he could match them all; but unarmed he might be quickly dispatched. They were protected by some agency around their land that never slept and always stood on watch. Even so, Zed had come through this magic screen. If he had done this, what could now stand in his way that he could not defeat?

These pretty, peerless enemies of his had youth, strength, and intellect forever. They had been matched and chosen as had he, they were like gods to him, but he could see their empty centers. He could see them as they really were, hideous, depraved, and wanton; superficial parasites upon a blighted land.

This tribe was long gone into a fall, but it did not show – yet. It was still awesome in its power, but so much less than it had been. He would prise open the cracks that ran through it, then wedge them farther, till he split the whole apart. If he had time. Time... time was running by his side against him in a race for his own life or all their deaths.

This recollection and review whirled through his mind as he stood gazing at the group. He was outnumbered, but he was a warrior, used to battle and fierce conflict. He loved a contest to the death. All the protagonists here assembled, even the magic ring creature, were not fighters; they had not the ways of killing. Even if they had the knowledge in their heads, it was not felt, it was against their mode, their principle of passive, slow, safe living. Why learn to fight when you cannot die? But Zed knew all the ways of war.

Consuella was conducting this investigation. He must be careful, as she would use this chance to speed him forward to the lip of death. It was an unhappy fact that she was enemy. She was fine, strong, and determined – a worthy mate for a chieftain like himself.

Everything here must be turned to his advantage. Every foe could become his friend.

Consuella was his deadliest enemy, yet she could be subverted.

Where Zed had stood before to entertain the commune with his life-memory, now he stood again.

Friend was in the forefront of the audience, and May was in attendance as Consuella began her lecture.

"Penic erection was one of the many unsolved evolutionary mysteries surrounding sexuality. Every society had an elaborate subculture devoted to erotic stimulation."

The audience was bored but looked sleepily at their new toy, Zed, with mild interest.

Onto the giant screen flashed a succession of bizarre sexual pictures. The couplings of ages, funny, sad, extraordinary, all heaving in various degrees of beauty depending on the time and culture from which they came. The watchers gave no sign of arousal; it was as if they had been formed sexless and inanimate long years ago.

"...But nobody could discover how this – became this."

Consuella poked her long pointer at the screen as a flaccid penis appeared there. She rapped it and it rose to full erection. Someone yawned, another scratched his nose and looked into the garden beyond the room. Only Friend was intent upon the experiment. Consuella was oblivious to them, as she warmed to her project.

"Of course we know the physical processes involved, but not the link between stimulus and response. There seems to be a correlation with violence – with fear. Many hanged men died with an erection. You are all more or less aware of our intensive researches into this subject."

One or two shifted uneasily under her gaze as if in memory of some past public humiliation.

"Sexuality probably declined because we no longer needed to procreate. Eternals soon discovered that erection was impossible to achieve and we are no longer victims of this convulsive, violent act which so debased women – and betrayed men."

Could this be true? thought Zed. Were they all so far removed from their true selves as to be just empty containers for their intellect? Had their skins' surface atrophied into a numbness? Could they not feel the inner quickenings of pleasure, loss, union?

"This Brutal – like other primates leading unselfconscious lives – is capable of spontaneous and reflexive erections. As part of May's studies of this creature, we are trying once again to find the link between erotic stimulation and erection. This experiment will test autoerotic stimulation of the cortex leading to erection."

May flashed a glance at the crowd in response to Consuella's words. A few stirred in anticipation; perhaps they recalled Zed's life-projection and hoped for something as exciting now.

Consuella passed the communicator ring over Zed's head and body and a line appeared on the screen, slightly oscillating, a visible reflection of Zed's sexual pulse. The watchers' feet shuffled as they leaned forward, the better to see the screen.

He was turned to face the screen. Images began to appear there.

Images which began to drive him.

Every imaginable aspect of sexual woman appeared before his eyes, and some aspects that he could not have imagined. Incessantly, in sequences and cadences, they flashed before him.

Remembering his reasoning before the lecture started, he realized that he must not act as predicted – the longer he could confuse them, the longer he would live.

May came over to him, and she began to massage his body.

The imagery grew in intensity, but he perceived a

mechanical background to all the picture sequences. There was an organization in them, they were clever repeats. He watched the line of his own response moving across the pictures like a ripple on a pool, steady and calming. He focused on the line – its evenness, its orderliness.

It was a projection of himself. In contemplating its quietude, he was feeding back still more calmness. The women behind the line grew in sensual ardor and convolutions. He held steady on the white line in front of the heated writhings.

May grew more attentive. He forced himself to breathe more evenly. He could recall some of the visuals. They were rerunning the program, a re-edition, but a rerun. He was steady. His body was stabilized from within. He was holding the Tabernacle back, contesting its power.

May signaled to Consuella. She walked between Zed and the screen. He looked back at her, unafraid. She would not dare to strike him in public, during an experiment, and so lose face.

It occurred to him that the Eternals all thought him to be as rugged as his exterior, a tough and active animal with no powers of thought.

It did not occur to them that he could reason.

Consuella proudly stood before him, and gazed right into his eyes. Behind her the screen had blanked of images except the line relating to his sexual pulse. That continued to trace an unwavering line.

Zed flicked his glance from her to the line and back. A thought crossed his mind and issued across his face in a brief smile. He could control his body. She still stood there.

Zed produced the desired erection for the benefit of the audience.

"Consuella's done the trick herself!" said Friend. They giggled, laughed, and applauded.

Consuella was the object of the Brutal's affection!

Consuella could produce "the reflexive erection," she was no better than the captive primate!

He smiled sweetly at her. Consuella flushed, enraged; but did he detect the shadow of envy crossing the face of May?

Consuella watched Zed sleep in his cage. She spoke into her communicator ring.

"The Brutal is now in the fourth hour of unconscious sleep. It is astonishing that Homo sapiens spends so much time in this vulnerable condition, at the mercy of its enemies. Is there any data on sleep patterns of primitive people?"

"Is that a priority request?"

"Yes. I will now test its working response to danger stimuli," Consuella said.

She reached through the cage, her hand like a talon, toward the deeply sleeping Exterminator.

Zed's hand appeared, grabbed her wrist. He was instantly awake and alert. She gasped at the physical contact. He released her.

"Does it please you to sleep?"

Zed remembered he had seen no beds here, nor yet any person sleeping.

He nodded. "Yes."

"Why?"

"I have dreams."

As she searched his face for meaning, the Tabernacle voice began to answer Consuella's earlier question.

"Sleep was necessary for man when his waking and unconscious lives were separated; as Eternals achieved total consciousness, sleep became obsolete and second-level meditation took its place. Sleep was closely connected with death."

Zed looked up at the night sky and its tiny points of light high above the rooftops.

Dancing glowing clusters of light. Spheres that rolled and spun. Darkness from which came spots of harmony. An enveloping warm blackness through which swam a curiously organic architecture.

"You. Your genetic structure. Your life chart." May's voice.

They were below ground again, deep within the pyramid, worshiping at the Tabernacle. May spun out a web of scientific litany before the screen, a homage to the rings' master. She had scanned Zed's body deeply with her communicator ring. At her command it had painlessly probed and captured Zed's design. His skin, blood vessels, muscle fiber, then deeper and smaller, into the cells and beyond them even into their components. Finally, his essential particles, the smallest plan within him had been projected onto the screen – for May's benefit and that of the eye that saw and projected for her. Might it not also record him for its own use? Did it scan all the incoming information and select the principal and most important for further use – as a line of defense and possible attack?

Using his military mind, Zed knew that whatever lay at the end of the invisible threads that led to, and joined up with, the center – the mystic spider web axis – was a silent, dormant king, plotting carefully for a confrontation and ultimate battle, its Armageddon.

Was it filing away his innermost thoughts as well as his physical details? To be sure, it might have most of him on file by now, but not his soul. Not yet, not ever.

"Look."

His eyes continued to follow the patterns as they ebbed and flowed before him. He struggled but could not decipher the images on the screen.

"You're a mutant. A second, maybe third generation. Therefore genetically stable."

The sentences came from her deliberately, slowly, as if they were thoughts confirmed and made real by her vocal admission. Like entries in a long-kept book. She was underlining and ticking off suspicions that had been written at the time of his arrival.

"Enlarged brain, total recall. Your potential is..."

She became speechless. Her arms raised as if to encompass smoke that grew and filled the room. She shrugged. She could not find words.

"Your *breeding* potential..."

"Breeding?" inquired Zed, leaning up on the slab.

They both paused, conscious that May had exposed a soft flank to him with those words. She looked at him with a frown, now on the alert.

"Arthur Frayn..."

He blankly looked back. His mind skipped a thought or two, then slid back to its shock point. Breeding – he could breed in the Outlands, it was his sacred right. Zardoz had decreed it so. He had felt it was a just and true reward for his superiority over others. He could only mate with those women who were as well-formed as he; no mutant female could he inseminate, no wild-witch creature could be his, only those of the design prescribed by Zardoz. Then the nagging doubt gnawed through and he felt the sickness that was Frayn's involvement. Was Zed just another life-form for Frayn to toy with? Had his love actions been part of a great gardener's plan, just a careful planting in the spring season, watched over from afar? Could his killings have been just the pruning and weeding for the same distant farmer?

Was he just a single barbed flower in a field of other special blossoms? Might he not be as grotesque as the mutants he abhorred? Was he not as strangely designed and perfected as they? They were the offspring of the random oneness that was life. Was he the product of a willful human reason – Frayn's? He must not betray these sentiments even to himself or he would weaken, and she would seize on them, securing them for her own use.

"How did you get into the Vortex? What is your purpose?"

He knew that she wanted him, however powerful she was. Her objective interest was aroused by his potential. Her body craved his.

"You're mentally and physically vastly superior to me or anyone else here."

Her eyes flickered. Zed sensed she was torn between the threats she saw and the potential she had uncovered. They were the same.

"You could be anything. You could do anything..." She wavered, then made her move.

"You must be destroyed."

Did she really feel this? If so, would she carry out her threat, and when?

"Why?" he said evenly.

"Because you could destroy us."

He breathed deeply. "As you have destroyed the rest of life? Can you unknow what you now know – about me?"

She thought deeply, then replied: "For the sake of science I will keep this knowledge from the others for the moment, keep you alive. But you must follow me, obey me, be circumspect, make no disruption, quietly do whatever work is given you. I will watch over you."

The meal rattled on as usual. All the Eternals were present. The evening light spilled from the mirror table back up onto their faces; it sparkled through the crystals set upon the surface.

The room was warm and friendly, the food simple but good. Like an elegant rich family, they bantered and teased as they ate; too spoiled to really understand anything outside themselves; too inward-looking ever to see themselves simply and clearly. Nonetheless, they presented a pretty picture to Zed as he assisted Friend, whose turn it was to serve the meal.

Zed never ceased to wonder at the elegance and fine detail of the place. The clothing, the cutlery, the shining skeins of cloth in the farther room; the beauty was confounded by the lack of appreciation in its owners. They acted as if it were their due. They looked but didn't see.

He moved easily, carrying the potatoes to and from the steaming kitchen, glad to be alive, fully mobile, able to move even in the humblest capacity.

He was functioning. Still alive.

Friend did not take to his chores so readily. Perspiring and irritated, he bit his lip and carried on.

Zed performed bis instructions to the letter. Each person approached from the left, a slight bow, the offering of the course; more? Removal of any dishes. Quietly, humbly, in rotation, each attended like the other, equally.

"Get a move on, you silly beast," Friend barked.

The others didn't mind Zed. They rather liked him. Especially the girls. They smiled and tittered. Zed calmly carried on. Consuella would be next; she began to tremble with revulsion at his closeness.

"Friend! Put that thing outside!"

She flashed her look of hatred at them both. An ominous silence fell over the table. Friend sighed, provocatively sweet.

"Anyone else troubled? Let's take another boringly democratic vote. Shall we... Consuella?"

Zed carefully proffered the potatoes to her from the left. The steam from them traced its way before her eyes, settled on her brow, condensed. She shook, but throttled down her voice.

"It's Friend's day to make the food. He must do it without help as we all do. It is fundamental to our society that we do everything for ourselves on a basis of absolute equality, and Friend knows that perfectly well."

Zed held a moist potato forward in its ladle, to her face.

"Yes or no!" His voice was strong.

She spun to face him, incensed at his interruption in the debate.

"Potatoes? Yes or no."

Everyone laughed, except Consuella. As it subsided Friend continued his dangerously sarcastic monologue. "Take a vote! I say get more Zeds to do the work. We have Eternal Life and yet we sentence ourselves to all this drudgery. I tell you. I'm sick of two hundred years of washing up – and I'm sick of pitting my bare hands against the blind, brute stupidity of nature!"

His arm flung out to the somber garden. The evening light had faded into malignant darkness.

The chatter subsided, the air grew tense. The battle lines were drawing firmer. Zed felt he should stop the confrontation, but could not do it. Consuella and Friend would have their final battle soon and one would be expelled and fall: Renegade or Apathetic?

Zed would be pulled down with them. He moved to May.

"You'd better do something about this."

It was her task to protect him now; they shared a secret which put her in jeopardy as well.

She nodded. He was valuable to her alive for longer than his sentence had to run.

"Consuella is right. Zed is being kept here for scientific study. He can earn his keep on the land, but he should not do the work of a servant."

Consuella would not pick up this hand of friendship.

"Time enough has gone to finish your study, May. Destroy it. See how it disrupts our community."

Could Zed detect a wider meaning in these words?

"It is almost over."

The agitation around the table proved Consuella's claim; they were disturbed, unserene. Out of character they looked quite insignificant and weak.

One girl spoke up.

"How can you speak like that in front of Zed? He feels – I sense that."

"Vote!" cried Consuella.

Friend shouted back, "Yes, vote!" The two extremists faced each other. The short, quick gestures of the Eternals' private language clashed and burbled with the noises of dissension. Bickering and bitterness were breaking through. Squabbles started again that went back to other days. Had Consuella and Friend once been as one? How could they resolve an eternal, fundamental division while locked forever in the same building? Old wounds were slowly opening wide.

The voting ended, one woman spoke; she had been the focus for the activity.

"May has been given seven days to complete her studies. Then Zed will be exterminated."

Although their voting process had been thorough, many still continued their confused debate. Zed was horrorstruck by the news, but had to wait his chance for escape. The Eternals' clamor rose.

Only Avalow was stable. She looked from Zed to May and understood.

She rose quietly.

Her hands began to hover and flutter in front of her; a long low note, more than musical, grew from her. The members of the commune became still and gazed at her. They quieted and grew watchful. The arguing had stopped.

Zed could feel that all were seeping into one unseen person, gradually, inevitably.

"The Monster is a mirror."

They all rose, almost floated to their feet, and their hands began to touch. Their eyes opened to see beyond the room and back into a general mind that came from all. Avalow was the initiator, the high priestess of their communion.

"When we look at him we look into our own hidden faces."

Their natural eyes were quite blind. Their bodies, empty vehicles.

"Meditate on this at second level."

Soft music issued from some. Others threw their transparent veils into the air so that they settled on their bodies, as if to insulate them against reality.

They were becoming one.

There was an exception – Friend.

He fought the communal mind, he still sat, and then spoke in a strangled voice.

"No, no, no, I will not go to second level. I won't. I will not be one mind with you. I know what May wants with Zed.

The Vortex is an obscenity... No! I hate all women! Birth – fertility – superstition. No, no!"

His words caused pain to the meditators.

They turned to him with their palms pointing to focus their thoughts onto him as he struggled. Their eyes widened, deadly and determined, as one. A great Cyclopean single eye. May spoke up; to stop him? Zed edged toward the window.

"Friend is beyond redemption."

Friend shouted, "No!"

"Friend is Renegade! Cast him out! Cast him out!" all the Eternals chanted.

Zed felt the invisible, tremendous, and unequal battle going on before him. The only outward signs were the stretched hands as they pointed at Friend. He seemed to buckle under waves of pressure, and fought back, trying to tear himself from a giant's grip. Then Friend pitched forward onto the table, dead or wounded by a ghostly paralyzing force. The crystal ring fell from his finger, plucked by an invisible power.

The Eternals turned to face each other, slowly lowering their hands, paused, then continued with their groupings. They turned toward one another and touched, becoming the same blind creature that Friend had refused to join, and which had smitten him. His eyes rolled up, his mouth sagged open. Zed moved to his side. He picked up the leaden head. It fell from his fingers and thudded onto the cold tabletop.

Zed sensed death – his own. He ran.

CHAPTER SEVEN

Doomsday Approaches

Zed ran beyond his limit. The multiple mind was too much. Here was a mystery he could not begin to penetrate. May's knowledge and intentions might now be known to all. They would vote him into instant oblivion, and were probably debating it at this instant. Could those looks really kill, or had Friend, poor lost Friend, been joking when he said, "Looks can kill here"? Might they be summoning up one long piercing bolt to catch him as he ran – or could they only stun what was in sight?

He pushed himself on; on and away from this place. Over the lush green fields, toward the edge of the Vortex. He glimpsed again the black bills edging the land through the trees; then, as he ran toward the Frontier, he saw the edge of life.

A scorched furrow, some ten yards wide, stretched along his line of sight. It separated the ashen wastes he knew so well from the green Vortex as certainly as a knife across a throat cut life from death. He kept up his stride as he ran toward this line: he might just clear it with a jump, for it was surely poisoned and fatal if touched. A familiar voice began to echo on the wind.

"Caution, you are approaching the Periphery Shield. Caution, you are approaching the Periphery Shield."

Then he felt a pull, as if he fell. Not down but back along

the ground from whence he came. It was as if he hit a wall, hard and final. Picking himself up he ran along the edge, feeling the pressure always pushing him back, with more strength than ever he or his men could have mustered. Even the wind was stilled by it. A prison without bars, glacial and perfect. He peered up to the hillsides, perhaps for the last time. His hunting ground no longer. Three riders came from the distant crest and stared down at him – familiar warriors. Zed raised his arm in a salute. The lead horse reared. They fired a bright rocket in greeting, then turned and vanished, impassive.

Zed slipped back through the trees. He could not escape, so he would attack. His only chance, however frail, was to do battle with the Vortex.

His men were nearby, but they might as well be a hundred miles away,until the wall was breached. If it did not fall, Zed would pull the Vortex down from the center – or die in the attempt. The prospect thrilled him. All the odds were stacked against him. It would be a fitting final contest for a great warrior.

He circled back. He followed the leafy path carefully from the side so as not to meet any traveler. It was not well-used. It was green, showing signs of overgrowth. He ventured out and stepped along its way, following the rising hill.

He slipped away from the path and circled in closely through the bushes, then darted to the huge window that ran along one side from floor to ceiling, catching sunlight. He was back at the Renegades' headquarters.

Inside the inky blackness, life stirred. Zed's view was marred by the reflections of the trees. He moved closer and cupped his hand over his eyes, pressing his face to the glass.

The old people were dancing. Slowly they turned, couple

by couple, around the ancient dance floor. One decrepit figure turned to Zed. His long bony arms slowly raised up and pointed at him; in recognition? The watery eyes and parrot-like toothless mouth quivered with the exertion. Zed felt stung, not as by an Eternal's punishing look but by pity for these creatures. Admiration, too, for they insisted on maintaining their ludicrous dance, keeping in step with time, apparently forever. He felt himself drawn to them and walked through the sliding door.

"I seek Friend. Have you seen Friend?"

They seemed not to hear him, but smiled maliciously back. Then there was Friend, dressed like the rest, but young. He turned. Half of his face had collapsed, sagging down in wrinkles, the eyes bagged, the mouth loose; even his hair was grayed and whitened on that side. His arm was limp, and the leg dragged. The giant had struck him hard.

"Friend."

"Yes." Friend turned to face Zed fully. "Old Friend! This is your doing!" He gestured to his ravaged face. The music stopped.

"Hear this, you old farts. Meet this creature from the world outside." Vindictive, cynical, he raised Zed's hand like a champion's. "This man has the gift of death! He metes it out, and he can die himself. He is mortal."

They crowded around him, curious and quavering; touching, fawning. An old woman tried to kiss him.

"Shall we give him back to death?"

The crowd screamed: "Yes!"

"Glorious death!"

"Yes!"

"Silent death!"

"Yes!"

They pushed closer now, not lovingly but violently. Pressing harder, boxing him in. He felt the horror of those old bones all around him and felt it would be easy to avoid them, but they crushed in with such vigor and ingenuity that he had to fight to get away. There were more to replace the first. Friend continued to whip them to a frenzy, and Zed was backed up against a wall, trapped, locked in tight.

"May, the scientist, wants to use him to spawn another generation to suffer our agonies!" So Friend knew of May's thoughts even as Zed had suspected.

They howled in futile rage at this. Despite their infirmities, or because of them, they tried to tear Zed down. They clawed and scratched, jumping on him, submerging him in waves of decrepit energy; venomous but antique. Zed thrashed around, feeling the old crones. More replaced the ones he threw off. Like hunting dogs on a wild pig, they would not quit.

He managed to fight toward Friend, and leaped clear of them. He suddenly roared with power, "Stop!" It thundered across the room. They shrank from him. He could not get out, he would go farther in.

"What is it you want?" he asked Friend.

"Sweet death. Oblivion."

For yourself or the whole of the Vortex?"

"For everybody. An end to the human race that has plagued this pretty planet for far too long!" Friend was almost poetic; at last here was something he felt deeply.

The Renegades had stopped to listen and cheered him through crackly throats.

Zed spurned them. "You stink with despair!"

"Yes!" Friend crowed.

"Fight back!" Zed countered.

The crowd applauded Zed as well as Friend now. Friend looked at him strangely while they cheered and cheered.

"I thought at first you were the one to help, but it's hopeless. All my powers are gone. They've even taken away my communicator ring."

Friend's spirits sank, but Zed shook him.

"Fight for death, if that's what you want!"

They were all on his side now, old but allies nonetheless. He had touched them in their yearning for death. This was the secret weapon; if he could bring them death or promise it, they were his.

"Where is it... the Tabernacle?"

Friend shook his head. "The Tabernacle is... we can't remember. How could that be?"

"Who made it? Someone must know how to break it."

"Yes... him." He pointed at the man Zed had first seen through the window. The bedridden man who had pointed at Zed so accusingly, so finally.

"One of the geniuses who discovered immortality. But he didn't like it for himself. He didn't conform, and this is what his grateful people did to him."

Friend bent down and shouted into the old man's ear, and prodded him with a stick. "We want to die! What's the trick?"

Again the old man looked toward Zed and slowly raised his index finger to Zed's eye. He smiled a toothless grin, then, wheezing, spoke.

"Death!"

The others recoiled, as if Zed had been designated Angel of Death by the Architect of Eternal Life. Zed held the old man's watery gaze and looked deep into his eyes.

"May might know," he croaked. "May."

Friend trembled with excitement. Zed turned and left to find the woman who might know.

Zed knew the grounds well, and dodging through cover, he quickly reached the house, unseen.

Some of the Eternals had drifted from the central contemplation group into other places of private reverie.

Zed saw May through the loom room window as he stole along the outside of the house. She stood silently among the many-colored hangings. Her body was awash with reflected colors from the skeins that mixed as he moved past.

Once in the room, he walked across the wooden floor, lifting layer after layer of gauzelike cloth to reach her side. Her body became more and more distinct as he approached, until finally just her own contemplation cloth separated her from the outside air, and his hands.

She was immobile within her silken wrapping, her slow and even breath being the only sign of outward life, a living statue in a forest of transparent tapestries.

He stood before her. Her eyes focused back from the infinite to the present.

"May, I want your help."

Without moving or acknowledging his presence, she spoke.

"You want to destroy us, the Tabernacle."

"I want the truth."

"You must give the truth if you wish to receive it."

"It will burn you."

"Then burn me."

He knew that this would be his weakest moment, for in his next step he would be within her power, in her total strength. If he took the step into the web she held up so invitingly, he would be lost for many minutes, he would be trapped and transported, his body a shell that could be killed in his spiritual absence. Must he step forward?

She smiled and beckoned him. A beautiful face; but what lay behind it? Could she turn into some haggard witch when he was in her arms, then snuff him out at will?

He had to trust her. She alone held the key to the last door. He knew she needed him more than she could admit now. She wanted him, body, soul, spirit, and seed. Would she mate, then kill him like some female spider and discard his empty body? He looked at her again. Her smile faded and her eyes lowered for an instant, then rose to look at him, unaffected by any design he could perceive other than her drive to make a new life from the old.

He paused, sucked a breath of air as if diving under water, then went beneath the surface of her rainbow veil. May moved and he was with her.

He went to her and was enclosed, enfolded by the patterned web. He felt a tingle run over his skin; from her, or from himself, or from the shimmering sheet he did not know.

"Tell me everything, show me pictures. Open your mind, your memory. Go back to the beginning, open – open – open."

He was trapped within the web. As a fly to a spider he had flown into the sticky center willingly, while she merely waited. She had expected him. There was no escape. Only her eyes filled his mind, the terrible piercing look which grew ever larger. He tried to hold onto the side of his consciousness but felt himself slipping back into the vaulted dark, sliding down into the dark mist of sleep she controlled. He fought against it like a shipwrecked mariner adrift with just one piece of timber for support. Just as those hands slipped off the floating wood, so his main-mind slipped away and down from his consciousness, and left it awash and solitary on the surface. No longer could he hold out.

Zardoz boomed: "You are the chosen! Go forth into the Outlands and kill!" The cruel wind bit at them as they screamed their eternal love for him. Their voices were puny as that same wind scattered the sounds across the plains to the mountains where the echo of their God still rolled.

May's voice, a dim dream, spoke. "Come. We've seen this. Deeper, further."

"Zardoz is our only God," he answered. "He moves in mysterious ways." He could just see her, just comprehend the game that she played, with him as board and all the pieces.

"But you lost your faith. Show me how."

He sank deeper yet.

The city street rattled with their comings and goings. A fine hunt this was. Galloping in and out of houses, around and around. The quarry was good. Young and determined, they fought back nowadays, not like the older times. These men had strength, some even carried weapons. They were no longer hideous manlike monsters, but like Zed had matching limbs; they were strong and fast but still not as strong and fast as Zed, still not so lithe and dangerous as he; how could they be when Zardoz was not theirs? The Exterminators who had fallen to the Brutals could look for no quick end. They would string out the death for many days with much rejoicing, but the weapons were the real source of celebration. To capture guns was their dream.

This made things more exciting for these exterminating angels. Murdering the aged, the passives, and the weak was just a chore. Now *these* were men. They pursed their victims farther.

The streets, like the houses, were littered with debris; they formed a cluttered stony dunescape with many intervening walls and rooftops.

"Zardoz gave us the Gun. We rode out. I knew the truth. Man is born to hunt and kill. It was enough. But something happened. It changed everything. I lost my... innocence," Zed said.

The street issued onto a large square, bigger buildings of many floors flanking it. In the center was the encampment of the Brutals. Here they would make their stand, among their rugged tents and children, where they could no longer run.

A light flashed in a window high to Zed's left. He turned and saw a face beckon, then vanish, a masked face, or a monster.

He slid from his horse and ran into the buildings, as his friends put the camp to the sword. He would leave them to their play. This game he hunted was more interesting.

He ran through corridors. They narrowed, grew thinner, spread and multiplied. They were walled with books, from floor to ceiling, book by ancient book. All musty, many damaged; some had fallen to the floor like bricks from crumbling walls. Here was an indoor city of old paper. As on the outside, there were open areas, like squares. Zed sniffed for the scent of man and stepped quietly through this labyrinth, over old volumes, past desks, searching.

A figure, the man he had seen before, stood briefly at the foot of wooden stairs. He beckoned Zed, then turned and ran up them lightly, into darkness.

Familiar with the art of ambush, yet intrigued, Zed stepped cautiously after the little figure. His gun cocked, he slipped quietly on and up. His killer-sense told him where the man was hiding. Now he had him.

The man was boxed into a dead end. Zed had him now for sure, stone dead. He raised his gun and centered the sights on the body, paused, then lowered the gun.

"Why did you spare him?" May asked.

"Something... I don't know," Zed answered.

The man was holding a book and calmly reading.

"Had you ever seen a book before?" she asked. "Never."

Zed glanced around the section they were in. The books were brighter and simpler than the others, their covers crisper. The book the man held showed pictures. He stood with his back to Zed, quite unafraid and absolutely lost in the strange pursuit of watching the pages. Zed crept closer. If this was of more importance than the fear of death, he must know it. He had seen men beg and cry and even laugh when confronted by the ultimate, but never this.

As he approached, the man stepped sideways, vanished in an unseen passage, and left the book to hover in midair.

This so amazed Zed that he did not pursue the creature down the maze into which he had fled. There was just the book. He touched it carefully and felt the thin wires that supported it and led up to the ceiling. There was no trap here. There was nothing primed to fall on him, or shoot at him – simply, this book.

An apple was on the first page, above it a sign, an "A"; on the next page a blue ball, above it another mark, a "B." Overleaf a tiny cat sat with its back to him, underneath a "C."

"You learned to read?" May said, following his vision.

"Yes."

How long did it take you?"

"Not long. I read everything. I learned all that had been hidden from me. The ways of the world before the darkness fell. Then I found the book called... called..." His voice faltered, caught in some strangled emotion, something too painful to recall.

Zed's enlarged brain had read with incredible speed. He had learned the manner of reading in a few minutes. He found that a book could be read as fast. His eyes could flick over the pages quicker than thought. All that he read stayed fast in his head. He sucked in learning as a desert in the first rain soaks up water, endlessly and without effort. He felt himself filling, brimming with new life. His whole existence slowly pivoted onto a new axis.

One book stopped him like a bullet.

"What was the book? What was the name of the book?" May was pressing him. She sensed this book's importance.

He ripped it in two and then into halves again, and again until the pieces were no bigger than snowflakes. He scattered them into the air, then clawed the dictionaries, the encyclopedias, the language primers, the mathematic textbooks, the histories from off the shelves and up into the air. A blizzard of paper whirled about him in his rage. He was the center of this storm.

Zed floated back to the room. May was pressing him close. He fought against her will.

"I don't remember."

"Tell me! Show me! You must tell me!"

He was being crippled by her eyes.

"I can't!"

It felt as though she would blind him, forever.

He twisted from her, yet could not resist her kind arms pulling his face to her breasts. She smoothed his hair.

"Tell me how you came into the stone."

"Don't know."

"Of course you know."

"I can't remember."

He felt himself beginning to suffocate underneath the cloth, inside her arms. He could see out, see into the room; but as at the edge of the Vortex, he was sealed within.

"Yes, you can."

He was going back in time again, back to the head, the grain.

"You knew that Arthur was Zardoz, didn't you?"

"No!"

"You killed Arthur, didn't you?"

Again he faced Arthur in the flying head.

"No."

"Show me the whole image."

Desperately he tried to hold back the image of Arthur.

"No."

He could hold it back no longer. It burst out of his mind. Again Zed shot him dead, straight through the body. Again he turned and smiled, this man who was coming back so soon from the dead, rising up, just as he was now sinking down.

Zed convulsed in the weaving room, racked with pain. May soothed him, smoothed him.

"You murdered your God... by accident... or was it an accident?"

Zed felt such peace that he was unburdened of the memory. The tight pain in his head had gone.

She smiled down at him and then purred. "Now... show me the book."

Catlike she cradled him. If he moved, her claw-like eyes sank far into his brain. There was a smile behind the eyes.

A warmth behind the cruelty, layers of good and evil in her heart.

His body responded as though possessed, jolted by her madness.

"The book. That book."

He ripped and tore it once again to shreds.

"It's all a trick! It's all a trick!"

"What was the trick? Tell me!"

Her eyes had damaged him. He was wounded. He could not resist. His head fell forward. He was exhausted, spent. The confession flowed out unstemmed.

"Zardoz said stop... said no more..."

The fields stretched out to the blackened edges of his landscape. Beneath the ashen, sterile earth, scorched and corrupted by nameless agencies so surely and so long ago, lay moist fertile soil, waiting for seeds.

Zed had overseen the planning and the digging. The prisoners worked in rows, until they died and were replaced. Zardoz had decreed it so. He gave them the special seeds, and only these would rise. They were from Heaven – Vortex; divine gifts to be revered, planted with prayer and nourished.

"Zardoz told you not to kill anymore.

"Yes."

"But to take prisoners."

"Yes."

"To make slaves."

"Yes."

"To cultivate instead of kill."

"Yes."

"To grow wheat."

"Yes."

"Did you need wheat?"

"No, we ate meat. We were hunters, not farmers. Zardoz betrayed us." "By now you knew about Zardoz, or guessed... That book."

"No."

"Show how you got into the stone. Show!"

Zed had been prepared. The others such as he were waiting. He had passed on his learning to them and they, having the same skills in absorbing knowledge, had grown with him to this moment. The head passed slowly over their bodies; they pushed their faces into the ground in homage and in fear of his coming.

They waited meekly. The rows of horse-drawn carts brimmed with golden grain; planted, grown, reaped, and winnowed according to the instructions boomed out to them from the head. It came now to collect its harvest. Now, Zed waited to invade the creature's homeland just as Zardoz had invaded his.

"Your friends were mutants too?" May prodded.

"Yes."

"You had a plot?"

"Yes."

"Revenge?"

"The truth. We wanted the truth," Zed said.

"Show it. What is the book?"

She had swooped back in his mind to the library again. The book he held was revealed. He could conceal it no longer.

THE WONDERFUL WIZARD OF OZ

WIZARD OF OZ

The heading shot up toward him in his memory's

eye. Then he cut forward, jumping in time to the moment he had entered that dark mouth.

Zed and his three comrades stood on the lips of Zardoz, whipping the slaves in to unload their baskets of grain. They filed in a loop from the carts to the center of the mouth and back again.

Zed nodded to his aides, then dived into the heap. They shoveled grain on to him; more grain was spilled on top of him from the slaves' baskets; all in a moment, barely interrupting the rhythmic shuffle of feet and the dry whisper of grain raining down. Zed was underneath, deep inside the cargo of Zardoz, a living part of the sacrifice they offered each season, ready to be transported to the God's home, the heaven known as "Vortex."

"I saw the trick," Zed said.

"So that was it," May murmured.

"Wi**zard** of **Oz**."

ZARD — OZ.

Zardoz.

And in his past, he once again covered the letters with his fingers to create the holy name from the title of a children's book.

Flashing forward, Zed relived the moment after they had left him in the head. He looked up through the grain and there was Arthur Frayn, speaking into his communicator ring. The voice distorted into that of Zardoz as Frayn watched, amused, through the crystalline eyes, the cowering audience outside.

"Zardoz is pleased. He will watch over you. Work hard and grow good crops and when you die you will go to the Vortex and live... forever."

"So that was the way of it. It was so long ago. Arthur's idea.

He called it that, a simple way of controlling the Outlands. *The Wizard of Oz* was an old story about a man whose amplified voice and awesome mask frightened people," May said, understanding it now.

"Until they looked behind the mask and saw the truth."

As in the book, so in the Outlands. Fearful gullible people had been cowed by shabby but extraordinary tricks. In awe they had worked for a charlatan, a jackanapes in god's clothing. He had bullied them and in exchange had given them cheap advice dressed up as religion, the while stealing from them, forcing them to live in uncertainty, using them to maintain his high position over all. Zed's life had been this man's whim. Under this yoke of superstition they could not progress to wisdom, to a freedom and a better understanding of the world, but they would always live in the darkness of fear, ignorance, and exploitation. Furthermore, they had to worship and obey. If he abandoned them – without his guns, outnumbered by the Brutals as they were – they would all be wiped away in days. Worst of all, Zardoz had turned them against their own race. They were genocidal soldiers – killing their own stock, spilling their own people's blood in the name of a foreign and grotesque alien cause.

Now they were used as a slave granary for Zardoz's kingdom. While Zed's people starved and died, Zardoz grew fat and laughed at them.

May had led Zed back into the real time of the room.

The past no longer flashed back and forth before his eyes. He need no longer fight to hold his sanity as his mind was whipped backward and forward at May's command.

"It was a cheap trick played on people's lives, to get your dirty work done for you."

"The rich have always done the same to the poor."

"A lie."

"Is the truth more palatable? I don't think so. History shows that superstitious religion is usually preferred to truth."

"Well, the truth is what I want."

"Truth or revenge?"

"The truth!"

"Truth or revenge!"

"Revenge! Revenge!"

He fell into her embrace as the last hidden words of his plot were wrenched out. He was a child again.

She kissed his brow and stroked his head.

"I remember feelings such as these... They stir in me."

He kissed her breasts: they shivered with anticipation as long forgotten sensations coursed back into her body, entering from him. There was a union between them.

May's eyes cast across the ceiling in ecstasy, then flicked down toward the door, troubled by a noise.

Consuella stood there, triumphant, blazing.

"So this is your scientific investigation! There's another word for it – bestiality!"

Zed rolled and turned, gaining his feet and moving toward the voice.

As he was set to pounce, she swung her gaze from May and shot him through with the deadly look.

He was jolted back across the floor through the hanging rainbow cloths, splashing showers of colored light in his wake.

"For this you will be aged fifty years," Consuella shouted. "No man or woman or beast will ever desire you again!"

Zed forced himself to rise. Weakened by May's ruthless

interrogation, stung by Consuella's shaft of light, he dragged himself to his feet.

She flashed again and he fell, but rose back through the waves of killing hatred that were stabbing at his brain from Consuella's deadly eyes. If he could not survive this ordeal, he would die – of this he was certain.

She hurled her most venomous thunderbolt of rage, concentrating all her force. He leaned into it and walked at her, into the blinding pain that seared through his bones and body.

May was astonished. Zed was surviving the worst that could be thrown at him. His powers were supreme. Consuella had cast enough force to stop fifty men. She was defeated. She wailed in frustration and, now, fear – an emotion these cosseted creatures could scarce recall.

Now he pounced upon her. Lunging through the hanging cloth that still cut the room into multicolored areas of light, he hurled himself at Consuella. The pain had desensitized him. He was a brutal animal again. He threw Consuella down and tore at her. May tried to pull him back. In their fall, looms toppled over and Zed was entangled in the skeins as the two women rolled away from his chaotic rage. He groped for them. May cried out: "He is blind."

"We can no longer control him," Consuella gasped. "Now we must become hunters and killers ourselves."

They backed away through the door and ran.

He stumbled in the ribboned winding sheet that entangled him. He could not see. Consuella's force had burned out his eyes. He heard someone approach. A soft hand took his and led him away.

It was Avalow. "Come," she said and guided him out of the room.

* * *

He was in the domed greenhouse that fronted Frayn's cottage, standing amid the trees and plants with Avalow. She had led him, almost blind, stumbling through secret pathways to this room that was neither indoors nor out.

Cool leaves and herbs were placed on his eyes to soothe away the pain.

"This will restore your sight and you will see better and deeper than you ever saw before."

Her beauty was too much for him. She was perfect, inviolate, unattainable, yet so close.

He raised a trembling hand to her, remembering the hard rules he had lived by in the Outlands. A new emotion rose in his chest. He was moved by tenderness. He felt compassion.

'I've seen men rape an old cripple woman in a wet ditch."

He recognized this new feeling as a weakness. She looked into his newly seeing eyes. She saw his future there. She paled and trembled.

"I see now why you are here. You are the one. The Liberator."

These were mysterious words, as yet beyond him. She appeared to come to a decision.

"I will help you if when the time comes you will set *me* free. You have great strength, but there are times when strength will fail you."

She broke a leaf from a musky plant and gave it to him. "Eat this when the need arises."

Zed placed it in a pocket. He felt renewed now from her ministration, but the new emotion had given rise to another – a bitter self-pity.

"This place is built on lies and suffering. How could you do what you did to us?"

Her eyes closed. She looked sadly into the past.

"The world was dying. We took what was good and made an oasis."

She took his hand and it was as if they had moved back to the founding of the Vortex. They were as ghosts, insubstantial, and unable to change events, able only to watch and learn from them.

They were at the Vortex edge, the periphery of the enclave. Eternals strode in groups, laughed, gardened, sunned themselves while outside on the other side, behind the invisible wall, hundreds of ragged people, Zed's forefathers, beat and scratched in vain.

They begged and pleaded and fell sobbing to the ground.

Men, women, and children – of all ages, all common in their misery. As poor as those inside were rich.

Insulated from the sounds of dying, the inhabitants of the Vortex averted their eyes from the praying, weeping remnants of the old and dying world.

Like dogs they threw themselves against the wall, unable to accept that they would be abandoned by so beautiful, rich, and educated a group as that which lived within the glacial enclosure.

Avalow spoke softly to him.

"We few, the rich, the powerful, the clever, cut ourselves off to guard the knowledge and treasures of civilization as the world plunged into a dark age. To do this we had to harden our hearts against the suffering outside. We are the custodians of the past for the unknown future."

The Brutals pounded hopelessly on the mighty wall. Its fragile transparency was contradicted by its strength.

No sound nor wind could penetrate its surface – yet air, light, and warmth flowed freely through it. There was one entrance high up to admit the Zardoz stone. There had been a time when this wall did not exist, so there would be another time when it ceased to be; for nothing that man built would stand forever.

The blossoms and the flowerlike Eternals walking among the peacocks and the statuary over neatly barbered lawns contrasted with the browns, grays, and darker tones outside the Shield. For the Brutals it was like a painting of Paradise; but no pigment, light, and shade created by a master could have portrayed a heaven so convincingly as this they saw. But other men, scientists, not artists, had built this heartless place that mocked their misery.

The Brutals beating on the wall subtly changed in form. It seemed to Zed as though they were now Eternals struggling to find a way in.

Zed and Avalow dissolved from the past dream-time back into their present. Their spirits reentered their bodies. Their astral frames flitted back to their own hosts and were one again. They were still within the transparent soft greenhouse, unprotected by reflexes or consciousness, and as Zed settled back into his body, his mind's eye still retained the Brutals' image as they threw themselves against the Periphery Shield. This jumped into a present picture, his reality. It was Consuella and a dozen men, beating on the insubstantial covering that made this tropical place. They had seen him and would crush the dome upon him with their fists and weapons, then beat him till he died.

CHAPTER EIGHT

Consuella the Warlord

The plastic sagged under the pressure. Avalow stepped back, her offered hand of help too late to save him as the structure shivered and caved in upon him.

The crowd surged forward like a wave against the semi-circular base, and drove and lashed the form again. They slashed it with their swords and knives but the thin membrane would not yield.

The material bowed in. A club, carried through the looseness, struck his body. He fell. The whole annex shuddered, groaned, then folded flat, tent-like, over him. He would suffocate.

Drawing himself onto his hands and knees, he tried to fight his way through, but the membrane, though clear as water, was as tough as steel.

Blows rained down upon him. His attackers were pressing the life out of him, squeezing the air from the canopy and out of his lungs.

He closed his right fist, placed it before his face, turned slowly onto his back, and concentrating his mind into his muscles as he had when Consuella sought to quell him, began to push against the membrane.

The plastic bowed before his hand. The attackers paused to watch his dying attempt against the impenetrable fabric.

Then they gasped out as his hand came through, slowly

but surely, into the lightness that was life. They stepped back in reflexive fear, and as they moved back, so he pushed forward. He ripped and tore his way out in a fury of ultrahuman energy. And like a snake that sheds its skin, he wriggled out from the embryo sac, leaving it wrinkled and empty in the litter of broken plants and containers that was once Frayn's experimental garden. As he stood erect, they lashed at him once more.

Darting through them, he ran to a cart, close by the bakery. Snatching a sack full of freshly ground flour, he flung it in the path of his pursuers.

A sheet of blinding snow-white dust sprang across the air between them, a screen behind which he vanished.

The Eternals lost their quarry within the blinding fog. When it was settled, he was gone.

No trace of him, no track, no slightly swinging gate betrayed his passing.

He was at large within the Vortex. Deadly and enraged, a proven killer of too great a strength for them to hold, he now ran loose.

Zed ran sleek and low to the point on the Periphery where he had last seen his comrades.

Many more were assembled there now; they gathered, waiting, at the invisible wall for their commander – Zed. He signaled rapidly that he had just six more days left to live, now less, and that his task was far from finished. Then he waved them back to hiding, for he heard the horses of Consuella pounding after him.

They melted back into the underbrush as Consuella, heading a column of pursuers, flashed along the narrow boundary of the wall.

She must have formed groups to race along arcs of the

circle that was the boundary. In this way she could cover the entire Periphery in minutes. Did she know he had supporters waiting in the Outlands close by the wall; or did she think he would try to get through himself in a last bid for escape?

He hoped it was the latter, for this would mean she still thought less of him, and hoping this, he bucked straight into the air and fell almost vertically down a long slope that no horse could follow. He might have jumped just before she came. His signaling, the withdrawal of his troops, and his escape might have been accomplished in secrecy. If she had been galloping hard and straight, the trees could have given him that cover, those extra seconds. He hit the ground at a run and took off, not wasting time to look back and see if she had seen him. She had patrolled the boundaries, now she would draw in the net, close in on him, and try to catch him once and for all.

He loped through the woods to the familiar walled enclosure of the Apathetics, the windows of the houses peering blackly through the stones. He paced along the wall, through the slender trees to the gateway, and skittered into the courtyard. He was just ahead of Consuella. They surely had seen him enter it. He hesitated and dodged into an opening.

It was the place where he had spilled the bread and thrown himself into a frenzied dance of life before the dead audience of the Apathetics.

Like people stricken with palsy, they were no threat, they were immobile.

There they stood, still lost in some subaquarian fog, moving toward him so slowly that he could perceive no motion of life as he panted hoarsely for breath, gulping in the air they barely breathed. He turned his back on them, pushed his face into the stone wall, which stuck wetly to him, and scraped his cheek around to look with one eye into the square outside. Consuella and her band were searching for him in the courtyard.

Turning, he saw that the Apathetics had advanced like animate deadly plants, somehow inhuman but man-like still. In the forefront was the girl he had embraced, fondled, and then thrown down in disgust. She opened her mouth and tried to speak. Horrifyingly they were all trying to touch him in a spidery, floating way, their arms like seaweed undulating in a deep-sea current.

Hooves clattered on the cobblestones behind him. Consuella and her troops now filled the square. A crackling of fire joined the clatter of their horses' hooves. She was burning the buildings, blindly smoking all the small game into the open in the hope of catching the man-killer.

The Apathetics in the houses were pitched or driven out under the legs of the hunters' horses.

Consuella had a regal, martial air which Zed now found himself admiring. Her hair flew back as she spurred her horse. The hunter, now turned quarry, recognized himself in his pursuer and was pleased.

The girl behind Zed reached out a hand and took a silver drop of perspiration from his neck, then put it to her lips. A tremor ran through her body. Zed glanced back at them. They pressed more closely to him, watching the girl's body change. She passed the sweat on to another pair of lips, a man's; he too tremored at the touch and passed it on again. Others took her touch and so a ripple grew into a wave that passed from the center to the edges of the crowd.

Smoke drifted in from the burning houses. The girl kissed Zed on the lips. "We – take – life – from – you." She turned and kissed a girl next to her, who kissed another, then they continued, kissing men and women in a second wave. The energy transmitted through them, melting the frozen limbs and heating their joints and muscles. Some began to moan as life restirred their blood. They clung leech-like to his body, wetly pressing their mouths to him, drawing out his essence through his skin. Like vampires on a struggling victim, they sapped him and he tottered, waited, fell almost, then lurched back, feeling for the magic leaf Avalow had given him. Incredibly, they were taking his life away. After all the dangers he had overcome, he was to die at the hands of these lifeless creatures. His fingers touched the crumpled leaf and he withdrew it, raised it to his gasping mouth, swallowed it, then fought for air.

The Eternals worked closer to his hiding place, attracted by the rising noise as more Apathetics fought for his person. They were becoming charged with his powerful psyche, and it rose within them and out against their sickly reason, into action. Zed felt his life returning from Avalow's potion, felt it burn through emptied channels, down thickening veins to his extremities. His life recharged again. He had survived once more. Consuella and two other horsemen clattered into the stone-flagged room and bayed out as they saw him. Zed turned and stumbled through another exit, overturning a cart to stop them following out into the courtyard, through the gate from whence he had come, swinging it shut, and – back into the forest, hounded still.

He glanced over his shoulder as he ran and saw the renewed Apathetics and Consuella's group collide in conflict.

Some were trampled, other Apathetics pulled Eternals from their horses; smoke rolled across his field of view, flames rose behind him as he ran.

The Vortex was fighting itself. It might be the first moments of a holocaust that would wreck it, if he lived to feed the fires.

Zed stumbled, lurched, and fell into a staggering run, his body kept going by his will and Avalow's knowledge within the leaf.

Daytime was sinking with his spirits. He was fading like the sunlight that caught him horizontally as he ran through the woods. His mind was failing. Just to keep going, but where he went was in some other's hands, or none.

In the darkness he heard strange singing and music. Little lights bobbed ahead of him like will-o'-the-wisps dancing in a marsh, and just as eerie, strange, and frightening.

The lights were carried by the Renegades, their heads bloated and grotesque in the lights. He swayed and saw they were wearing masks and fancy dress, perhaps in celebration of the burning of the buildings. They shrieked and danced and cackled around him. He was too tired to fight now. They had him.

An old man prodded at the slack figure. "It's him! It's him!"

One dressed as death bent over Zed's fallen form.

"None of them could catch him – but he falls into the hands of the poor old Renegades."

Zed spoke in a whisper, up into the ring of faces enclosing him. "Death! I can bring death to you all! Find Friend! Take me to Friend!"

"What's he say?" an old woman asked.

"Shut up!" another answered.

Zed tried to see them as they had been. These wrecks were once the best of Vortex life – vigorous, alert, and brilliant. They were the only people now who might help him through.

If they could just raise the veils of senility and see him as a mirror image from their own past.

They gnashed and twittered over his head in some unknown private quarrel and debate.

He closed his eyes.

He came back to the present time after a spell in total darkness, a dreamless crypt, to find that he was walking. He felt his strength returning with each stride. The little lights still danced around him. Now he was part of the procession which had stumbled upon him. He walked with death. He was her bride.

The sly Renegades had dressed him in an old bridal gown, a veil covered his face. Through the lacy gauze he saw sharp patterns of new light. Fire on torches carried from one bonfire to another. Flames licked and fed around him. All the population were giddily drunk with old memories of violent times refreshed by fire.

Passions were erupting through the still and stoic modes that had once held the Vortex firm. Stupefied with excess, they reeled around him, as if the world were being tilted back and forth, shaken at its core.

Through this welter, the Renegades led their stately, wicked little march. Death had Zed's arm; he patted it, and grinned up through the patterned net. Zed saw an old sparkle in the young eyes, flaring in the crumpled face; times remembered, deeds done.

Zed looked about him with mounting horror. The gaps were widening, the implosion would occur. Some Apathetics had trapped an Eternal in the bushes and were stoning him to death, their laughter drowning his screams. Couples made passionate love to each other in the light of fired houses where trapped people raged. Madness reigned.

Young and old laughed, danced, killed, and made love with a mindless hysteria that shook even Zed, who had lived through, led, and initiated worse deeds himself. Could he be weakening in his resolve to destroy, to kill the center of the state?

An old man bent down to two ex-Apathetics who rolled in each other's arms.

"It's a miracle. We're Apathetics."

He crackled, "Tell us how. Please. We want some too."

Still in love-throes, the Apathetic explained, "We started chasing the Brutal. We got excited. We saw someone. We thought it was him."

"It wasn't, but we killed him anyway," added her partner.

"Then we felt desire," the first explained. The infectious violence had stirred dead sexual longings.

Zed glanced up to a tree silhouetted in a rocket-flare that burst and briefly hung before it fell to start a low fire in the fog-damp woods. A body had been crammed into a forked branch, like a big cat's killing. Eternals hurrying past were caught in the pale red glow of the flare, their shapes picked out with guns and swords, and they all hunted only him.

Death clawed Zed's hand in his.

"Look at all the excitement you've caused – you naughty girl."

Dawn was breaking on a vastly changed Vortex. Dusk had left the Vortex sitting orderly in its light, smug and secure. Now the Vortex of the dawn looked a hundred years forward into the ruin of time's hand; or could the place have been ravaged by a brutal senseless army of the night? Looted, raped, and ravaged, the fabric of the commune burned, but the steel heart still beat safely underground within the inviolate pyramid. The dead would rise again as surely as the sun. Doubles of these corpses, breathing lightly and smiling, would rebuild the chaos into the once-stable hell that smoldered here.

Death and bride approached the house in a stately parody of a marriage march. Consuella, her horse turning and wheeling, shouted orders. Zed saw her, martial, proud, and beautiful. Then he, too, felt the return of the old martial rhythms within him. He was recovering. He was back.

Consuella spoke up, her voice exciting him to combat. As she stirred her soldiers, so he, too, was roused to fight. "Your task is to secure all arms and weapons. Cut off food supplies. Work house to house. East to west down the valley. If you find the Brutal destroy him immediately. He's trapped. It's only a matter of time."

And you're trapped, too, he thought as he looked up at her. *You and I are both locked together like two poisonous scorpions in a green bottle.* He reconsidered. No, she was the head of a wolf and he was a secret deadly insect in her hide, who would bite into her veins a paralyzing poison while he drove her mad with irritation.

The system fought itself. He had been "seen" a hundred times that night and "killed" a dozen more. Old feuds were being settled in the name of law and order. If he could only strike one lasting blow to the vitals – to the brain – all would be his. This damage about him now, fearful though it was, was only on the surface. He must get underground to face his final dragon.

Consuella turned her horse, wheeled, and nearly rode over Zed, who stepped back to let her gallop by. He felt the whisk of her whip as it cut down on the flank, smelled the steam rise from the horse, and she was gone. A ringing clatter in the street hung for a moment, then was spent like the gray wall of smoke that rose a hundred feet over all the Vortex! A death veil, suspended in mid-air.

"Friend! Friend!" Death took Zed's hand and led him to the man standing before the doorway of his workplace. Zed smiled at his ancient colleague in a resigned way. Despair haunted Friend's features, but his masklike face could not conceal a deep delight in what went on.

"Kiss the bride, dear Friend. Kiss the bride."

He let himself be shouldered, nudged, and worried up to Zed by these mad old infants. Death lifted up the veil, opened his eyes wide, and barked a new laugh back at Zed's strong face.

"You did well," Friend whispered. "I will take the bride. Death comes closer for us all. Find May. Tell her Friend needs her."

The limping procession turned away, aping the exit of the troops. Friend gripped Zed's arm and led him through the doorway of the museum and down into its maze-like heart.

May picked her way through the serried ranks of statuary toward them. The monumental clutter of Friend's cavern looked neat now compared to the slaughter and rapine of the surface above. Zed's gun hung from her fingers, low against her body. She stepped out into the living area, the unfamiliar weapon balanced in her hands. Her finger ran along the barrel and down to the chamber and the bullets as she looked at them both in turn.

"Friend, I cannot sanction this violence and destruction."

"It's too late, May. There's no going back."

She pleaded with him, with the revolver as a pivot and a threat.

"Don't destroy the Vortex. Let's renew it. A better breed could prosper here. Given time..."

"Time! Wasn't eternity enough?" said Friend.

Zed spoke at last. "This place is against life. It must die."

His words fell with a terrible finality. May trembled, wavered, then passed the gun to Zed as a token of her agreement.

"I have my followers. Inseminate us all, give us your seed. In return we'll teach you all we know, I'll give you all I have. Perhaps you can break the Tabernacle – or be broken."

Friend clasped May's hand and joined it with his in Zed's. A triple pact.

A triangle against the circle of the Vortex.

Friend: "An end to Eternity!"

May: "A higher form."

Zed: "Revenge!"

CHAPTER NINE

Exchange of Powers

The three conspirators stood in the center of Friend's arena, the curtained place leading off into countless passages that looped and struck out into rows of memories.

Statues, paintings, badges, costumes, weapons, jewelry, bric-a-brac – solidified moments from the past. Friend had had a near-insuperable task, but had made inroads into the accumulation of centuries within which he lived. He had made passages through piles of crates. Simply moving them into related groups had taken many years. Then the opening of the crates, the cataloging of the contents and the correlation, all this long before he could draw conclusions from this collection of monuments to man's diversity. These conclusions from the past, gleaned from the evidence of long ago, what of them? Perhaps that was why he had become so cynical, so despairing.

However, here would be a good place to teach Zed, and Friend would make a good teacher and a better guide through the sum total of the past. They were underground, behind stout doors, well protected at the center of a maze.

May and her women were the objective teachers. Each one was a messenger and communicant with a special branch of knowledge. Individually they would give Zed weapons of knowledge with which to fight the dragon. Physics, chemistry, mathematics, linguistics, philosophy... each woman, in turn, had insights that branched out in other realms with which to arm him for the battle, to help him hunt the Tabernacle down.

Like Zed in the Vortex – a needle in a haystack – so, too, the Tabernacle was hidden in the finite volume of the community.

A half-sphere extending from the highest point of the force field – circular like the peripheral edge of the land and Vortex – was Zed's and his quarry's ground. The Eternals hunted him – he hunted the Tabernacle.

The force field might extend underground into a sphere. Zed might be locked into another round world. So – he was trapped inside an invisible globe.

This globe extended high above his head and far below his feet. At the center was the author of this force and next to it was Zed. The only way to penetrate the wall was to strike at the center. First, Zed must equip himself like any other warrior with the special weapons needed for the fight and all the information with which to find and kill his prey. Then he must hunt, kill, and dispatch him. The walls would fall, and the breach complete, his confederates would pour into the city and kill the population, level the buildings, and withdraw, their mission over.

He was the spy within the citadel, but he had been exposed, caught, and sentenced, and lived now on stolen time.

There was not time to prepare or search. Brilliant though he was, he could not absorb all the necessary skills. It would take years of study and mental exercise. No one man could scale those heights. Time had defeated him. Another invisible and relentless force had caught him. Time – that was the key. Allies he already had.

Friend was an implacable colleague, as filled with hatred of the systems as Zed, his purpose the same as Zed's: an end to this place. May's bargain would be honored. Zed would inseminate her and her followers and direct them away from the attacking horde that would sweep in from the west when he had blown the walls. They could ride out into the wasteland to begin a new existence and a new world, nurturing the life within them. With their combined strengths they might repopulate the land, and if by some mischance they were all killed, then so be it. It would be Nature's choice. May wanted life from him. She would not fail him either; though time might.

This musing passed through Zed's mind in an instant, then his thoughts were shattered by a dull booming from above. Consuella's gang were at the door.

Zed spoke to May. "How much time do we have?" He knew that there was none.

"We will not work in time. We will touch-teach you. You will take our knowledge by osmosis, out of time. Your mental powers are greater than any of ours. With our knowledge, you may accomplish what we have failed to do."

It was the dangerous but inevitable way for her to take him. They would guide him and bathe him in their knowledge, so that their minds would mix through the touching of their skins. And as he mated, so would they pass back to him their own seeds of information that would grow in him, as the life he transmitted would grow in them.

A mystical, sexual binding would wrap them all into one astral level, apart from the world, outside of the lengths of natural time. It would be fierce for one so untutored in the arts of mediation and bodily perfection, but there was no other way for them. So, taking his hand, she led him to her woman, who had been waiting quietly unseen, hidden in the museum.

They laid him down, and like petals enfolded him. Science, religion, philosophy, and art, four monumental zones through which to ride in a moment stolen from time's breath. It could not be enough, for they could not represent all areas of fact and fiction, art and life. Though they could not give him armor in full, yet they could arm him well enough – if he could stand the madness that might come from leaving time again. Each Eternal had practiced and evolved slowly into higher dream-places where time flowed in and out like the tide. It took a hundred years of study and devotion. To plunge him deep into the most dangerous reaches of other-time yet again and expect him to take the jolts of input knowledge might be fatal.

That was their risk, the chance they would take. The stake was high; so were the odds. They had just one dice throw with which to win. He had been used, his memories displayed before their gaze. His secrets had been driven and drawn from him. He had been taken back in time to see the beginning of this place. Now at least he would be given pictures from the lives of others. He would be replenished with strong thoughts, detailed and well constructed in their design. An architecture that had grown tough through the tests of time and other men's inquiry.

The Apathetics had nearly drawn his spirit, his life-force, clean from him; the times to come would help replenish him.

The Eternals had battered on his body and chased it raw. The women would rub soothing balm into his muscles while he slept the waking-dream.

He looked around at the velvet curtained area, his silken couch, then felt their touch and was transported into a continuum of space and time that stretched out like a flat zig-zag road across a black nothingness, a road on which he moved, random, unrelated, lost.

Characters from other languages grew up before him. Words were chanted in many tongues. The patterns of many languages forming dazzling shapes across his face, the music and poetry of words from the ends of time surrounding him.

The women rolled across and around him. He felt adrift in space – beyond any gravity or help he knew. Other views poured across him other times. His central mind absorbed the endless information. His frontal, outside thinking could not comprehend the traces as they flashed through, for all was too fast and rich for his conscious comprehension.

It was a rich fabric interwoven with too many strands at which to clutch. The tapestry's pattern and color were too vast for him to view. He was too close to the weave.

The women were massaging him, mounting him, and he them. He felt their bodies and their minds as one, as they felt him. Where the Apathetics had touched there was the pain of loss; where these women touched was the joy of gain. Images dazzled his eyes. Amoebas, soft and pliable, grew and danced in dimensions undreamed of, enveloping him within their gelatinous mass. Geometric palaces grew in scale and intricacy around him, filled with numbers and circuits that flashed on and off with changing lights.

The women's bodies grew larger; then their flesh dissolved to show their bones and workings; then they changed to diagrams of life, which fluttered back to ancient delineations of man's body, the lineage of life; then ran forward to the present, and once again he was engulfed by the pleasing presence of the female force, whole, firm, and warm. He looked with a new eye. The blinding light did not hurt, it filled him. He glowed, all his veins fluoresced, each one alive with new growth.

He was taken high above the earth, then swooped back into its deeps. Into the center of molecules, then back out into deep space to look down at his own infinite smallness. And all in ecstasy. Warriors refought wars through him. Campaigns that lasted a century ran through him in an instant. Music rang through him as a parade of notation, and reverberation echoed and multiplied in his system: all his body was one live harp.

Colors, for their own sake, grew from one white light, split into primary lines, wove themselves into dazzling pictures which grew up and around him, towering above him. Then they shrank, and he was amazed by their smallness and intricacy and his own gigantic size.

He walked the earth again, from the beginning of time. He was all men, all women, from the past, come forward to one moment. He fell across huge gaps, black chasms that could lose him, as a white spark of light. A lightning bolt of life. He could be the source, the darkness, the electric bolt, and the flaming target, all at once – and was.

The pulses flowed through him, from his head on down. He bucked in pleasure as they rippled through him from the hands of the women by him. He saw that they were all parts of one being. He thrust into them, each in turn. He penetrated their bodies. Their orgasms burst like sun-flares before his eyes, each revealing a new light, other carnal knowledge.

Replete and shimmering, the group that was him and May and her women seemed to part for an instant. The sexual, sensual communion ebbed and waned. Its peak past, they coasted over a review of their loving labors. They moved together as in flight over a mountain range built of intricate, jumbled white-and-colored scaffolding picked out with jeweled points all set on a black sea. There was no scale to judge it on; they flew over the highest peak, and the darkness faded up into daylight slowly through gray and grainy lightness.

His body still hummed with the resonance of that first time away from now.

The women rested too. They had been before him as more than a group; they were all parts of one larger creature – the Vortex. Each one, like parts of a robot body, had been chosen at the outset as a special partner with a unique function, to work in harmony with another. Each one had a special part. As apathy had set in, so specialists had fallen away from the main body, leaving gaps in the process. This meant the reserve skills of each had been pushed forward. They had been stretched. When the Renegades had begun to threaten the static system, their expulsion had meant the best, most oblique minds had been lifted from the Vortex; thus even more strain was put on the remainder. It left only the orthodox, and they more overstretched than before. A core left to cope with mounting extremism. This single being (built though it had been with resources more than needed and endowed with an ample reserve) was overstrained.

It was trying to split up and re-bud. May and her group would be the cells in this living organism to take it out into another place. The Tabernacle was the artificial nervous system that ran the news from one section, group, or individual back and forth across the geography that was the Vortex, the organism that was the commune. Therefore, it was not a central brain, for that would have made it king here. It was a network of knowledge lines intersecting and crisscrossing as the occasion demanded. A different foe from the one Zed had imagined; not a giant, but a legion.

His rage rose up uncontrollably and it seemed he was in the Tabernacle room, the place that was the womb of this being, the place of regeneration for the Vortex body. Did the Tabernacle lurk behind these walls? Zed fired his gun blindly at them. But no bullets splayed against the surface. His shells were empty. The hideous rebuilding figures in their soup of life grinned back.

Then May, pressing on the other side of him cried: "The Tabernacle is indestructible and everlasting."

They shook him out of his dream. He was back on the couch. They caressed him, still hungry for his body, awakened from their centuries of glacial frigidity.

Friend entered the curtained room, the tent-like zone where they had renewed the mind of Zed in exchange for new life.

The flash of nightmare had passed through Zed and he was relaxed and back into real-time before he plunged once more through space. He landed on the long flat strip of road that ran from time's end to time's beginning over the blackness. Loop on loop flowed in its own pattern, freed from the gravity, the pull, of one-way time.

Friend passed his hand across Zed's eyes and they were both swimming down to the lost road again.

It was near the beginning of Vortex history. The Eternals, in their separate cocoons of silk, sat in the contemplation room where Zed had been displayed. The contemplation aids were augmented by the hollow tubes of silk within which they sat. They could be visible to the rest but detached from them until such time as their minds returned.

Friend and Zed, as ghosts, strode among them. Some

Eternals talked to each other in a litany of learning. Endless games of skill and strength from history and the mines of chance were played back and forth with lightning speed. Debates and information flowed back and forth evenly and lightly. Zed and Friend moved forward in time to the same room, years ahead. Now, more Eternals had taken to contemplation. Finding that the exchange of facts and further study had not opened any new doors, they had turned in on their minds in search of spiritual perfection. Astral travel was the only means for distant exploration. Avalow was growing in this manner. To other Eternals, much of the traveling was simply magic-carpet riding, empty and vacant and passive, as the pictures rolled beneath them. Later these became some of the Apathetics. Others, seeing new routes and changes that were not allowed, became disturbed and, finally, Renegade. They could see too much; others, not enough.

The contemplation room was low-lit and voices rose around them. As the ghosts of Friend and Zed faded from this past, they surfaced like tiny silver bubbles racing to the surface of a pond, and burst into the present.

Friend spoke. "We have come so close to penetrating the mysteries, only to find our minds are wanting. We wanted to solve all the problems that had betrayed men, but we just weren't up to it."

Zed nodded. "I see one creature. A blind monster condemned to Eternal Life. Rebuilding itself from fading plans."

Just as a human body's cells grew old, and as they died, were copied, letting flaws and smudges be reproduced – these in turn turning out to be grainier and more defective pictures of the last – so here, the Eternals, when rebuilt, became paler shadows of their former selves, until the paler shadows begat paler copies yet and the shadows melted back into sunlight and oblivion.

But how were they linked to each other and the Tabernacle? Friend took him back again, to the beginning, and down they sank. A stately scientist, in real-time a babbling Renegade, the one who had pointed at Zed that first time, was standing at a slab, on which was May, her forehead open from a deep incision. In his fingers was a clamp and at the end of this a tiny crystal which he set into the wound, saying, "This crystal shall join us, each to each, and all to the Tabernacle." And each was ceremoniously loaded with this third eye of light.

So, all the Eternals carried this tiny transmitter which beamed out their every experience to be recorded in the Tabernacle. When they died, they were rebuilt from their plans, starting from a tissue record. The accelerated fetus was programmed with all the life-experiences of the dead person up to the moment of death so that he would step into his place in the Vortex, alive and the same as before.

The old scientists had started it. They had done it. Friend explained. "They were the scientists – the best in the world. But they were middle- aged, too conditioned to mortality. They went Renegade. We were born into Vortex life. We are their offspring. We were better able to deal with Eternal Life."

The Renegades raged and ranted, sad remnants of their earlier glory.

As Zed watched, Friend dissolved them back to an earlier time; their faces and bearing changed, making them into more stately and proud creatures. The chief scientist was on a platform with the others; he faced them in the room.

"We seal ourselves herewith into this place of learning. Death is banished forever. I direct that the Tabernacle erase from us all memories of its construction, so we can never destroy it if we should ever crave for death. Here man and the sum of his knowledge will never die but go forward to perfection."

The initiators of the place, the builders of the commune, had deliberately hidden all knowledge of the building of the life-lines so it would be doubly secure against attack, even from themselves.

When they had built this place, the times were desperate, the world and all its people sick with more than fear. The holocaust, like the returning flood, had drowned all except a few, who, prepared like clever Noah, had floated safe on its crest in the isolation of the Vortex. But having sealed it tight against the storm, they'd locked themselves inside forever.

"It's a prison! It's a prison!" Zed cried. He was lying on the couch in Friend's room while Friend, like a doctor-teacher, sat at one side sagely nodding among his clutter of past times and promises of moments yet to come.

Friend was relaxed as he counseled Zed. It was as if Zed were on a voyage undersea, with Friend afloat to help him when he surfaced and look down when he was swimming in the deeps and see him through the glassy stillness, distorted by the liquid of time's change.

Zed pulled strongly through these places and absorbed all that he met. He was not a passive traveler, so much amazed by the newness of the sensation and so dazzled by the beauty of the sights that he became awash with mindless joy. He was proud, alert, and unafraid – like a captured barbarian chieftain being taken through the imperial capital. And he was like this in more ways than one, for he was in the center of all that he had fought, but would not bow his head in homage, rather preferring to watch, learn, and wait for an opportunity to strike. Although outnumbered and enchained, his spirit was supreme. His clear eye never flickered in fear, always roaming over the new landscape, always learning.

He had perceived that the Vortex was a prison and the Eternals were locked inside its walls forever. If they behaved they could look forward to hundreds of years of the complex interplay between the men and women and the power groups. Slyness and remorse, wit and wisdom were constantly being replayed and reordered from their limited numbers. They were all in luxury cells. The disobedient were aged down into darker dungeons. Those who killed themselves were brought back to play the prison-game again. The weaker souls whose minds had seen the true conditions and lacked the will to change became sickly Apathetics, consigned finally to oblivion. Yet there was no jailer, just the process, the Tabernacle which ran this dread place. To think that Brutals had tried to gain entrance here, convinced the beauty they saw was real and so desirable!

This prison was most cruel in its complexity. Friend interrupted his thoughts, reading them.

"It's a ship. A spaceship. All this technology was for travel to the distant stars. That was why they developed extended life and the anti-gravity devices – the flying stone head."

"Did you go?"

"Yes, another dead end. Some are still out there traveling into the void."

This was another voyage that need not concern Zed's present tribulation.

"I need time," Zed muttered.

So it was an ark, set adrift to await the ebbing of the flood. It was planned to settle somewhere and restart the Earth, or if the waters never receded, to sail on forever, drifting helplessly, yet thriving within. Other ships had gone out to the stars, to perpetuate the problems of humanity on far-off planets. There was no knowing if they landed safely or not. If they had, they would still be faced with their own essential natures as well as the new problems of the fresh planet.

The reviving system which brought them back to life here was for spaceflight. If these ships were voyaging light-years, and they would have to get to the nearest stars, they would have needed this eternalizing machinery for their crews; all specialists, all parts of the ship's control, bound each to each and all to the ship – by a Tabernacle.

The whole ship enclosed in a wall through which they could see but which would protect them from meteors and other bodies that might attack them – hence the force field around Vortex. The force drawn from gravity itself. This was how the head had flown.

The mediation, the communal mind – to keep them spiritually strong and bound together.

The zoo in which Zed had lived was to repopulate the island-planet on which they landed. Tough stock from which to breed new lines.

So – the Eternals were like monastic navigators, living lives of hard work and spiritual exertion, meditating and perfecting their mental skills, until such time as they could land and colonize. This Vortex in which Zed now stood was the control. If this, the home model, was in decay before his arrival, then the others would be showing equal signs. The basic design was at fault, the flaws were inherent in the plan. The link was left behind here on Earth, a vehicle moving through space as fast as its brethren. An impermeable satellite, level with Earth's surface – the time-ship Vortex.

Consuella's guard smashed the battering ram into the

door above. They hammered the wood against the barrier with rapid strokes, but down below, the rhythm of the beat was infinitely slow and booming.

May and her women had elongated time for Zed. By speeding up their living rate, they flew through time like rockets, making the outside world seem sluggard. Nonetheless, Consuella's troops were nearly through the door and there was little real time left.

Avalow had entered through a secret path and stood before Zed. She gave him another token for his strength – a crystal much like the ones implanted in the Eternals' foreheads long ago, but much larger. Offering it to him, she spoke:

"Now we have given you all that we are, one gift remains. It contains everything and nothing."

In their minds they swam toward each other through the blackness of no-time. Jewels sparkled in the darkness, some a million miles away, of huge dimensions, others so small and close they brushed onto their skins like stardust. Dewy opalescence, pearls of petals of emotion and experience slowly shed to show the ripe center of pure feeling, glowing from his touch to high horizons. Entwined as one they flew headlong, trailing stars in their wake like a comet's tail, over cliff-tops that yawned a thousand miles below their flying bodies. They interwove their limbs and climbed like one great bird soaring on the hot gusts of sweet desert air. It wafted them on perfumed breezes miles high above swaying violet plants that beckoned to them through an invisible sea, their tendrils of unspeakable lengths and complexity. The tendrils flowed with the essence of life and the fliers felt them, sudden scudding changes shuddering them back and forth. A melodious whistling from the great speed filled their ears and sang in to their hearts' center. As they touched, they endlessly cavorted and spun in the current of ecstatic space. Penetrating and interpenetrating each other's flesh, they glowed with each other's touch. Delicate fingertip touches sent them up and out, the smallest movement a herald of great floods of sensation. Always they mounted upward to one supreme moment, which became in turn just the foothill peak of another, vaster range revealed by a parting in the cloud layer. Then this in turn was peaked and yet another height was calling, up and on to new snowy peaks of softness. Pleasures were almost painful, time stretching out and on. Avalow had been pure for three hundred years, now the inviolate child-woman was at last penetrated. Instants dilated to centuries of experience that wiped away all thought and drove behind memory in its intensity. Fondness, love, lust, insatiable hungers were quenched, then were renewed and replenished by unimagined fulfillments, yet welcome and familiar as new friendship. Cadences of pleasure undreamed of, bodily sensations beyond imagining – yet always strong and certain, straight and shining in their intensity, moving into the divine whiteness of the sun's center – a cold flame that consumed and renewed.

Zed was back in the liquid deeps once more. Avalow preferred the jewel as May had the gun. It lay in his palm.

"Look into it. You will see lines running into the future. You will make insight-jumps. When you can see into this crystal, then you will be ready. Only then."

As he touched the crystal, it flared with light, burning his hand, and he was back in Friend's room.

Zed looked into the gem and saw only his face, multiplied and quizzical. His other selves gazed back at him in an echelon, rainbow halations shining around his many faces, like haloes around a pantheon of rogue saints. But nothing more could he see in it; no clue.

His reverie was disturbed by a faraway voice. "I have come for you."

Zed jumped to his feet, gripping the revolver in one hand and the crystal in the other.

"Over here," the voice cried, luring him on.

Zed crept toward the voice, down corridors of stone men and bronze women to a place of costumes, where wax figures waited, gorgeously attired, for a homage that would never come. Many figures stood about him, dummies clothed in costumes of the ages, kings and queens and courtesans. A jarring reminder to the Eternals of the Earth's past. No doubt these had been intended to be preserved in a museum at some landing place; or perhaps it was just booty, looted quickly before the world fell into disorder and collapse; or maybe it was a reminder of the follies of power that had brought the world to this pass. The voice had come from among them. The dead faces looked the more sinister for their emptiness. Zed slid through, gun forward. A white-gloved hand touched him as he passed. Zed turned to face a tall figure, dressed in a top hat, cloak, and evening suit. He ripped at the bland face and pulled away a thin rubber mask.

"We've met before, I believe."

The face was round and smiling, the small beard bobbing. It was Arthur Frayn.

"Frayn!"

"Come now. My Brutal friends call me Zardoz."

The smile faded. Zed looked into the eyes and they searched him with madness. Too late he saw Frayn's hand fly up below his breastbone. Zed saw the knife blade vanish into his chest, but did not feel pain. The shock of knowing he was dying hit him like cold rain. Caught off-guard by a trickster.

"Revenge!" cried Frayn.

Zed gripped the knife as Frayn released the hilt, smiled, turned, and was gone. He pulled out the knife – the blade twanged back; it was a joke, a stage-knife. Another of Frayn's games.

"Now we're even."

Frayn had reappeared at the end of the row of figures. He might be an illusion, so Zed thought, and cautiously watched him, still gasping from the shock of his mock death.

Arthur snapped his fingers and a glowing ball appeared in midair. He threw it from hand to hand, a spinning glass sphere.

"Would it have been worth while. To have bitten off the matter with a smile. To have squeezed the universe into a ball, To roll it toward some overwhelming question, To say: 'I am Lazarus, come from the dead...'"

Zed was shaken. Zardoz had returned, and old fears throbbed through him. He trembled.

"Do you know the next line? It's T. S. Eliot." Zed replied.

"'I am Lazarus, come from the dead, Come back to tell you all, I shall tell you all.'"

"Well done. Well done. You've learned your lessons well."
"What will you tell me?"

Arthur laughed. He tossed the crystal ball to Zed.

"What do you see in the ball?"

Zed peered into it as he had the diamond. He saw no solution there.

"Nothing."

"Then I have nothing to tell you. But I will show you tricks. Conjuring tricks."

Colored skeins of silk appeared from his clothing and then from thin air. He plucked them like magic flowers, out of nothing. Flags and scarves flowed from nowhere, and all the time he laughed. Zed found himself smiling too. The absurdity of creation hit him. Arthur spoke.

"Good. You see the joke. One must see the joke! The cosmic joke!"

Frayn was gone, leaving Zed with yet another gift, or clue, a crystal ball, to join with the gem and his returned gun, to form a trio of aids.

Consuella and her companions were now inside the museum, raging throughout its depths. Zed was protected by the interior lines of defense that wove around him, the network of corridors and the gigantic area with all its strange occupants and forms. Friend had made a frightening maze that few could penetrate. The tunnel buffered Zed from his pursuers. The statues rocked as the group of maddened Eternals ran wild among them. One stone man tottered, fell, crashing to pieces. They yelled in delight, and took it for a signal, beginning to destroy the statue's neighbors, until the pathway they were in was filled with broken fragments. They had covered their tracks behind them, so they became lost in the deepness of the vault, unable to find their way back to the entrance. The carefully preserved art treasures were being pillaged and vandalized like a desecrated tomb.

All this happened with great slowness – the statue falling forward was caught by the hands of slowed time and gently laid down onto the floor, where it slowly cracked, the pieces lifting out into the air with the beauty of a flower opening. The wreckers ran on pads of time softened from speed by the mind of Zed's helpers.

He could still think of his gifts for just a little longer as the raiders closed in on him. Now they were splitting into small groups, ravaging like rats through the place that was once Friend's preserve and only empire, scuttling through it, destroying all before them.

Zed sat in the center of Friend's room, upon an upright chair. He faced a small table and looked calmly at the gifts he had received: the gun, the gemstone, and the crystal ball. The answer lay within these objects.

He had to solve the mystery, but sensed there was one piece missing, another gift perhaps.

Consuella quietly walked into his room. She strode up behind him as he sat with his back to her – deep in thought, too lost in the unraveling of his puzzle to listen for a footfall.

She carried a long dagger at her side. His neck came into reach as she continued to close in on him. His head bent forward. She raised her knife hand until the blade flashed above her head. At last he saw her, reflected in the globe, but did not move. The knife hovered above him, whether stopped by her own hand or some other agency he could not tell. He made no move. He would let fate decide. She could not strike.

She spoke at last. "I have ached for this moment." She tried to prolong her instant of joy, but it somersaulted over into remorse and defeat. He turned to look at her.

She dropped her hand down. The knife fell to the floor. She followed it to his feet.

"The hunt is always better than the kill." Zed put down the gun which he had held before him.

She looked up at him.

"In hunting you, I have become you and I have destroyed what I set out to defend."

"'He who fights too long against dragons becomes himself a dragon' – Nietzsche."

"I am not like the others. I would fill you with life and love."

She took off her communicator ring and put it on the third finger of his left hand, the finger on which all Eternals wore it.

With this gesture, she resigned her position in favor of his, joined him in action, and awarded him equality with her. She recognized his powers. He looked at her, then at the ring, and back to her again before he spoke, savoring the gift, the gesture, and all its meanings.

"You have given me what no other gave – love. If I live, we will live together. Go now."

His mind returned to the tabletop in front of him; the revolver, the gemstone, the crystal ball.

Now a new gift – Consuella's communicator ring – was set beside them and he was lost in new thoughts. She stood, shut out by him, then turned and was gone. The velvet hangings that made a door and concealed Friend's living quarters moved slightly as she passed.

Outside there were other voices, bayings and shouts in the darkness. She called to them in the voice of their commander.

"The Brutal is not here. I was mistaken."

A respite.

Zed picked up the diamond and brought it close to his eye. It was many-faceted, cut by an expert to allow for maximum reflection and refraction. Someone had cut this stone from a dull pebble, to reveal its present shape. He picked up the crystal ball and held it between him and the gem, the globe acting as a magnifying glass.

"Refraction of light... infinite..."

White light could be broken into many other kinds of light, into many colors, some of which man could not see, all of which could bounce inside this most shiny and hard of all objects. The toughest, most everlasting form could only be destroyed by one of its own kind grinding into it. It was the most reflective and refractive of objects on Earth, made from carbon, one of Earth's most common elements. Carbon crushed with immense pressure miles underground had been formed into this diamond, the key to his search.

He looked into the communicator ring and spoke to it.

"Tabernacle, what are you?"

It lit up, glowing softly, but no pictures came, only the voice.

"Not permitted."

"Where are you?"

"Not permitted."

"Do you know me?"

"I have your voiceprint, Zed, and your genetic code, but only fragments of your memory."

He held up the diamond for the ring to see.

"Tell me about the crystal transmitter."

"I cannot give information which may threaten my own security."

Zed looked from the crystal to the ring and spoke in answer to his own question.

"Brain emissions refract low-wavelength laser light passing through the crystal in the brain. They are a code sent to you for interpretation and storage. Yes or no?"

The Tabernacle paused before it spoke, an uncharacteristic hesitation, a change in its smooth process.

"Not permitted."

Zed continued to describe the nature of the Tabernacle, trying to lead it into the open, into a confrontation.

"A receiver must be like a transmitter. I think you are a crystal. In fact, this one. This diamond."

He held the diamond closer to the ring.

"In here is infinite storage space for refracted light patterns."

He waited for the reply. It came at last in a form that betrayed humanity and humor.

"You have me in the palm of your hand."

"But you could be elsewhere?"

The Tabernacle could move across space, projecting its information from one base to another. In this way, if one diamond were attacked and crushed it could fly safely away before the end. There might be thousands of gems within the Vortex. An attacker could never destroy them all, even if he could find them, for many would be buried. Yet the entire Tabernacle had flown into the diamond which he held in his hand. He had drawn it from its lair. Many refuges were all around for the light that knew everything. The battle-proper would now begin. It could destroy him, and there was no guarantee that, even if he died, the light that was the Tabernacle would be obscured, dimmed, or extinguished.

The space within the diamond was crowded with millions of wavelengths, from all the spectrum and beyond; waves of energy – from dark radio light up to the blinding white light of the sun – shimmered and were buffeted inside the tiny glacial container. At last he could see inside it as Avalow had predicted. He was here, pitted against the entire wisdom of the Vortex. It had chosen to be with him. It could have lain far away, safe and sound.

"Yet I choose to be here."

"Why?"

"To confront you. Already you have learned to see my

light wavelengths in the diamond. Now you will try to erase the reflections and destroy me. Your aim is to destroy me, isn't it?"

"Yes."

"Would you kill God?"

"Such vanity."

"I am the sum of all these people and all their knowledge..."

The battle was beginning. Zed could feel the seductive pull of the creature as it tried to lure him on.

Its voice broke into two, then three, and then a dozen, then a hundred. The Tabernacle began to plead for the Immortality of all the people that were and ever had been. Their voices lifted in a begging chorus, pleading, entreating him.

The diamond glowed with revolving colored lights that danced hypnotically before Zed's wide staring eyes.

"I am all-seeing. I am everywhere and nowhere. That had often served as a definition of God."

The symphony of voices multiplied into countless choirs playing to Zed alone in some weird cloud-swept hall. The colors in the diamond reached out and enveloped him in skeins of light that swirled about him, binding him in color.

"Would you destroy us and all that we are?"

Zed's own voice startled him. It sounded like a man from another time, but it pulled him from his dream and into danger.

"I must."

The visions hesitated but continued in their rising cadences.

"Would you not be part of us, joined to us, a light shining to the future? Love us, cherish the truth..."

All so seductive, Zed's resolve was weakening; he was slipping, dissolving into the stone. Then he shouted, "No!" and all the beautiful illusions vanished sharply.

The Tabernacle had tried tenderness. Zed had not

expected that kind of attack, but had survived it well. What would it try now, how would it next venture out of the stone to fight him?

That was his mistake. The diamond did not venture out to him. It plucked him down into itself. Like a pike reaching up from the bottom of a river to take a moorhen chick that looks up to the sky for its attackers, it came from the least expected direction, swiftly and surely, its jaws snapping shut around its prey.

The diamond had vanished from his hand. Zed looked up to the enclosure in which he sat. Everything felt different. He ran across and touched the walls. They were changing. They were hard and glassy. The illusion of the room dissolved as he beat on the shiny panels that once had been exits into Friend's underground province.

There was just a hard shiny interior all around him. Either the Tabernacle had grown around him, or it had shrunk him down to a microscopic size and swallowed htm whole. It did not matter which, for both were equal in their finality. He was still whole and functioning, but so was the Tabernacle. The possibilities could drive him mad before the battle started. He closed his fears shut, checked his gun. That was solid enough. If they battled in a dream or in reality, there would be only one being at the end of it.

The Tabernacle spoke again.

"You have penetrated me."

Zed waited for the walls to move in on him, for ghosts to leap out of thin air. He did not think to look down.

CHAPTER TEN

The End of a Beginning

The whole room was in black glass; the floor slowly opened and he fell deeper into the center of the diamond. He had just been in one tiny facet of the surface. He was sliding through all the many other facets to the middle of the stone. He would be surrounded by an infinity of reflected light, trapped forever in a three-dimensional maze of ice and fire.

There was no fingerhold; he clawed at space and sometimes jarred off buttresses that loomed from the inky blackness and then vanished once again.

He tumbled over and over in black space, lost and doomed.

He tried to think himself upright and stable, and in doing so, found that he was on his feet.

Beneath his feet the blackness became a flat glass floor, substantial and supportive. So – the Tabernacle was reading his ideas, trying to destroy him with illusions, but falling back, giving in, giving ground. If he could disbelieve what he saw, he would survive, but he must erase the reflections and destroy; mere survival was not enough. He must still get to the real center of the storehouse.

He pushed on, solidly believing in his quest for the true and living center of the stone. Most of all he revived the passion in his mission. Light grew around him and he found himself in a new pattern of spaces, each one bounded by mirrors that flickered with light.

The floor stretched flat and on forever. The ceiling, likewise, and the walls had the same quality of glassy stillness that buzzed with low light pulses.

He groped among the unbalancing screens, for each one looked as though it were a corridor, and each corridor looked like a screen. He crashed into them and stumbled from wall to wall, but on and in. He felt it was only quite a small volume, cunningly engineered to seem vast. His calm center was stable. His central mind was still.

Whether fantasy or reality, this room would be the last battleground. Figures appeared in the distance, then all around him: May, Consuella, Friend, Avalow, somehow apart from him, unreal but by his side. He touched one as it ran behind the surface of a screen. It was an insubstantial image, and as he touched it, it slowly wiped away. There were more. Consuella and May came close. He made himself erase their beauty, though it hurt him more than he could stand. He heard their agonizing cries as they were rubbed out. Now if Consuella died, dead she would remain, May too. He clenched his teeth and carried on, regardless of the cries for help. Friend fell, then the Renegades and Apathetics, one by one. All fell away into the final darkness. Their loves and hates, their precious minds, the storehouse of the best brains of the centuries, all consigned, like him, back to the real time from which they came. The voices and sounds jumbled and rose into an uproar like a whirlwind battering on his ears. They could not fight him back. His heart was cold, his mission near its end. At last they were still.

The Tabernacle spoke. "We are gone. You are alone."

Then he saw his final opponent, one to match him well and equally.

It was himself. His own memories and times spent here

were now coming back to him. His chance for immortality and harmony within the Vortex was rerunning. The reflection advanced up to him, gun in hand. Zed ran, backing away from the final confrontation, colliding with mirrors and walls. He was routed by his own person, his returning past.

His calm middle-mind came into his consciousness, soothing his desperation. Why was this the final phase? The Tabernacle would save its best chance till last. If he could win here, all would be over.

Zed was real, the other Zed he saw was a flat image, brilliant in its construction but false, only a colored copy in light.

Zed must face himself. If he could face the truths about himself, he would be free. His past deeds, his true person – if he could stand and take them, it would be finished and he could go forward. Not as he had been, but as he now was.

Why hadn't the Tabernacle killed him with a bout of energy? The answer was clear. It could not take life, but it could dissolve his wits until he destroyed himself. Suicide was the Tabernacle's only weapon. It could drive him mad and lead him to self-destruction, but it could not pull the trigger.

Was Zed about to kill himself if he shot at his own reflection? Could the Tabernacle have convinced him that *he* was just a mirror image? If he pulled the trigger, would he stop the bullet and be killed?

If he shot the gun at his reflection, could it be that the bullet would cut into his own self?

The Tabernacle could not kill. It must have been a prime directive at the inception of the Vortex, that was sure. Now – what process was the Tabernacle using to drive him to self-destruction?

It must be a perversion of a method it had once used for good. It must be one based on a meditation method, evolved to assist the Eternals to see themselves as they really were.

This was true.

Around him more and more memories from his past came up to haunt him.

Once again he rode and killed. He fought with Consuella and May in the place of weaving. The Renegades dashed at him. The Apathetics drew his life from him. All rushed him at once on the multiple mirrors that enclosed him.

The Tabernacle was a teacher, inevitable, benign. A force for good, in spite of its own survival directive, a monument to its designers. More and more memory images came up. One central one! Zed the Exterminator, lean, brutal, deadly. He faced the new Zed, a man filled with knowledge that held compassion and disgust at killing. Zed had to pull the trigger into his own reflected face, or the old Zed might shoot him first.

He slowly raised the gun until it pointed at the eye in front of him. He squeezed the trigger.

The images grew more violent and eager to overwhelm. Then the percussion cannoned off the walls like thunder, the reverberations echoing and reechoing through the halls. The bullet pierced the glass, blood oozing from the crack. Zed watched his own past dying. The Exterminator fell with the shattered glass into a pile of mirror shards at Zed's feet.

Within Friend's museum chaos reigned. Consuella's group had long since left, but there were other Eternals, undisciplined and heady with looting and destruction. They laughed and shouted as they wrecked the treasures, like drunken soldiers pillaging a defeated city. They ruined and desecrated the priceless objects, smashing and ripping in a mad reversal of all reason. And still they searched for Zed.

"He's here somewhere. Search everything!"

"Smoke him out!"

Deadly, hungry fires began. They cut into the dry atmosphere with relish, cracking and leaping from timber to timber; consuming crates and paintings, tapestries and costumes, faster and more completely than the mob.

In Friend's quarters, Zed was slumped over the little table. The diamond was in his hand, the globe in front of him, the ring beside it, the gun in his right hand, spent cartridges around it. May and the others started forward to him. They had watched Him through the time of battle as his body had been racked with tensions while his mind fought the Tabernacle far from their gaze. Then he had fallen forward. Smoke sneaked into the room, voices followed. Friend shook Zed.

"They're here." Zed did not move. Friend spoke to the others.

"Take him to the east door."

They dragged him off away from the looters, but those from which they ran were only one party. Friend and May's women were backing into another group, just as deadly, and moving in from the eastern door they sought. They would all surely die. They had been seen and recognized. The attackers advanced, grinning, and shook their weapons, ready to destroy.

Friend looked to Zed for help, then sighed.

"It's too late, he's finished!"

Consuella stepped out of the shadows. May looked at her bitterly. Consuella shook her head and stepped up to the limp body of Zed, gently kissing his eyes, infusing love.

Zed awoke, got to his feet, conscious and alert. He faced his aggressors. His hand stretched out to them in defiance. They halted.

He spoke to his followers.

"Stay close to me, inside my aura."

The attackers slowly began to retreat as Zed advanced. Smashed statues sprang back to their pedestals and were remade exactly. Torn paintings mended themselves. The mob fell back, running backward with the weird certainty they would not fall.

They ran back up the east staircase, Zed following, the diamond held high. The others close to him were amazed at what they saw. Zed had reversed time.

Then, suddenly, time snapped forward again and the mob ran down the steps as they had done once before, they smashed the statues and the paintings just as they had done before, exactly as they had done. Then they passed the ending of their time-reversal and found themselves sheepishly confronted by thin air.

Zed and his party were safely aboveground, breathing fresh air again underneath the sky.

Friend, May, Consuella, and the rest surrounded Zed and looked at him in wonder. To have reversed time and led them through it was beyond even the furthest abilities of Avalow.

May and Consuella embraced as May bid her goodbye and went to prepare for her departure.

Friend cautiously approached Zed, as if he were a different person from the one he had taught and known. The master was now the pupil.

"Can you tell us how things stand? What next?"

Zed looked at him as if he heard a far-off voice.

"An old man calls me. The voice of the Turtle is heard in the land."

Then he walked to the place of the Renegades.

Zed stood beside the bed of the leader Renegade, the man who had begun this experiment that was the Vortex. He was weak and spoke softly.

"I remember now how it was." The Tabernacle having been destroyed, the memory of its construction had now returned to him.

Zed held the diamond before his rheumy eyes. The old man fixed upon it and nodded.

"We challenged the natural order. The Vortex is an offense against Nature. She had to find a way to destroy us. Battle of wills. So she made you. We forced the hand of evolution."

He wheezed into a near laugh that became a death rattle in his throat. His eyes stilled. Zed closed them with his hand, then stood silent for a moment before the dead scientist. So, Nature had evolved him to undermine and vanquish this place. The founder of the Vortex had just died – Zed had won.

"A good death," he said, in homage. His peace was broken by cries of joy from Friend, who had just realized that a natural death for a Renegade meant the Tabernacle had ceased transmission.

"You did it!" he cried delightedly.

The man who had played death stepped forward to see for himself. "He's dead," he said to the other Renegades who crushed around to see. Then they heard a rushing noise from high above, the head was falling.

The massive and enormous stone head that had defied gravity for so long had finally given up the unnatural struggle. It was plunging to Earth, the wind screaming around it.

Those gathered in the Renegade hotel saw it flash past the windows. There was a rumble as the ground shook, then the crashing sound waves hit them.

The Tabernacle was well and truly defeated. Things had come to an end.

The wonderful beginning that had been the Vortex was slowing to a halt.

If the head no longer flew, if the aged could now die, the wall around the Vortex must no longer stand.

Zed strode across the lawns away from the dying rebels and toward the house. It smoldered but still stood erect. The sun bounced off the domes that surmounted the contemplation room, but as he looked at them, they flashed full of fire and vanished into air and smoke.

A strange unearthly voice called him and all the survivors. It was Avalow. Zed, like the rest, picked his way over the wounded who littered the lawn to a silver pool close by the house. Set among palm trees and flowers, it was just in sight of the black Outlands against which the Vortex had so long stood safe and unafraid. Avalow was at the center of the pool as if she had just walked over the water to attain her central place. She sang and beckoned them all to join her. Eternals, Renegades, Apathetics wound their way to her. Disheveled and limping they came. May and her women all on horseback waited in a lane nearby; they were clothed for travel and hard weather. Pack mules brought their baggage. Zed looked up at May.

They waited at the foot of the giant tree, the ancient cypress, in which Zed had first seen the Eternals meditating, only a few short days before. The house seen in the background through the branches, the lawns, and the strolling people had had the calm and promise of an everlasting golden age.

The peace that reigned over them had seemed quite certain for a thousand years.

Now, all was changed. The house still stood, but was in ruins. The smashed windows gazed out like skulls' eyes on scenes of desolation. The lawn was littered with the wounded. A battle had raged here. A civil war had rent this city-state to ruin.

The artificial equilibrium that had been established here between the Vortex and the outside had suddenly swung back in favor of a natural order. This artificial paradise, inset in the real world, making its surroundings the poorer because of its presence, had been swamped, flooded back into the Outlands. Now all the goodness that had been artfully stored here would be redistributed back into the places from which it had been stolen. May and her women would set out. Her caravan stood fretting in the shadows of the tree, horses' hooves pawing at the litter of pine cones and needles. Zed took May's hand.

"Ride east. You will pass through the wall in safety." He handed her the diamond which had been his key. "Let your sons and daughters look into it."

May tried to speak, long-forgotten emotions rising up in her. Her pulse quickened. She was torn between duty and feelings of more than love for this stranger who had smashed all that had been her life yet refurnished her with passions and new purpose.

"What will become of you? Will you go back to your people?"

Zed shook his head.

She wanted to leap down by his side and never leave him. Behind her the column of horses moved restlessly. Just as Zed could never rejoin his tribe, so she had to lead this expedition into the wilderness to begin a new race. They were committed. He could never again be with his people – until death might unite him in some spirit world, if such existed. She had to spearhead a new tribe that she would never see. They were both in mortal time. The seconds ticked life away. Forward, always toward the ending of their lives. They shared a moment of mutual sadness.

Zed broke in on the silence. "I've come too far. There's no going back for me."

He walked up the bank, past the tree, and toward the silver pool.

May jerked the reins and her column trotted away into the ending of the Vortex and the beginning of the Outlands and new life.

Zed did not look back. His army was attacking from the western edge and thus would miss May if she was lucky. If they were not all wiped out, they would have a hard winter to survive alone; a brief time before the birth of their children; then greater risk as they would be doubly vulnerable. But some would not bear children, and they all had had two hundred years of study and exercise to prepare them for this time. They were the strongest and most clever people of their age. They were many. They would be a match for natural hardship. Zed envied them. They would be the first to land from this ship. The first explorers to set foot on a new Earth. A tiny party scratching a bridgehead on a hostile planet, with only will and knowledge to help them. But what an iron will and what massive knowledge!

Zed was nearing the pool's edge. He could see Avalow standing on a pedestal in the center. Magically, she was dry, having reached the stand in some miraculous way. A last demonstration of her sublime powers.

Her call continued.

Around the corner of the house, as if in answer to her, came the last remnants of the armed searchers, still wild for Zed's blood. They saw him and began to cheer and run at him in a desperate last charge.

Consuella moved forward from the group of watchers by the pool and raised her hand. They halted, recognizing her authority. "That's useless. It's all over." She waved them back. They fumed, then, crestfallen, joined the people at the pool's edge.

Friend called to them: "The Renegades are dying like flies!" He delighted in the progress of death, like an invisible bailiff claiming his dues with spreading swiftness.

Consuella spoke to them all, pointing at Zed. "He's not to blame. We destroyed ourselves."

The remaining weapons clattered to the ground from the Eternals' hands. Avalow's chant grew, and they were drawn closer to its power. Arthur Frayn plucked at Zed's sleeve as if to impart a witty piece of gossip to him which he had saved up to this moment.

"That's truer than you know, Consuella. And here I would like to claim some credit if I may."

They looked at him in surprise and disbelief. He was delighted by their attention and savored it.

"You see, our death wish was devious and deep." He turned to Zed. "As Zardoz, Zed, I was able to choose your forefathers. It was careful genetic breeding that produced this mutant, this slave who could free his masters."

He made a sweeping gesture that included all the Eternals and ended with a bow. Then he pointed at a familiar figure in the crowd. "And Friend was my accomplice!"

He laughed in pleasure at the discomfiture of his watchers.

They were too dazed with fighting and pillaging to attack him in revenge. They were beyond all feelings of bitterness now. Arthur turned his impish attention back to Zed.

"Don't you remember the man in the library?"

Zed recalled the dim face and overlaid it with the grinning one before him. The memory and the present intermeshed, fading into one person.

"It was I who led you to the *Wizard of Oz* book."

Zed's face was stony.

"It was I who gave you access to the stone. It was I! I led you! I bred you!" Arthur almost hugged himself with delight. He would have clapped himself on the back if he had been able.

Zed swiveled to face him. "And I have looked into the face of the force that put the idea into *your* head. *You* are led and bred yourself." Zed had seen the force that led them all. All were designed; the will made them separate, but their oneness joined them.

Arthur and Friend were delighted. The irony of Zed's statement filled them with laughter. They looked at each other and spoke like twin children blurting out a secret.

"We've all been used!"

"And reused!"

"Abused!"

"Amused!"

By now the song of Avalow had permeated the group so secretly, so surely, that they were all part of her song. The melody rose. A farewell chorale of praise and pain, a last celebration of their powers, a greeting for their new, last life. The Eternals moved into their familiar single mind and talked at a deep level, as one creature. For the last time, their minds entwined, their souls joining into a communion.

Zed could not be part of their sublime happiness. He stood alone and looked west.

Avalow led them. She drew their music to a peak, then effortlessly spun it into one single note of her own, releasing the others from their meditations and melodies until she alone had the single sound, then this too faded into silence.

She looked at them and raised her arms, as if in blessing.

"Death approaches. We are all mortal again. Now we can say yes to death, but never again no. Now we must make our farewells to each other, to the sun and moon, the trees and sky, the earth and rock – the landscape of our long waking dream."

She turned and faced Zed. She was vulnerable, trusting.

All eyes were upon him. She mutely pleaded for death from him. Her arms raised in entreaty.

"Zed, the Liberator, liberate me now according to your promise!"

He raised his gun, but could not pull the trigger. Consuella was at his side.

"Do it! Do it!"

"All that I was is gone."

His hand shook and fell as he spoke.

A shot burst across the air. Redness blossomed at Avalow's breast, she swayed as a sigh of happiness came from the watchers. They threw their hands into the air with joy as Avalow fell into the pool, shattering its stillness with her beauty, her blood spreading out into its waters.

Eternals crowded around him, not knowing that another had killed her.

"Kill me next!" a girl begged him.

Arthur spoke to Friend. "Let's kill each other, Friend. Have a proper regard for irony." He thought for a moment, and with a flourish produced a white bird from thin air, saying, “One last trick!”

Friend applauded.

Exterminators were in the tree-line, firing into the Eternals. Their horrific masks were a sad comment on the fallen head of Zardoz that lay hidden in thick woods a hundred yards from them. Shots spattered out.

Friend took Arthur’s hand. They looked around for one last time. Friend took a bullet and fell. “Success! It was all a joke.” He paused. “Is that all? Ah... it hurts.” And with that, he was finished.

Arthur toppled.

The Exterminators ran out from their cover across the lawn, putting the dying to the sword, with expertise finishing off those who still lived. The Eternals thanked them as they died.

Zed took Consuella’s hand and, bent nearly double, ran zigzag through the crowd toward the thick woods nearby.

The Exterminators were baffled by being surrounded by their willing victims. The bodies lay across the neat lawn, their bright clothing and distorted limbs looking like a ravaged flower bed. The killers, their masks giving them cruel, dead gazes, continued in their task.

High above, at the east end of the valley, at the lip of the rise, May stopped her column, pulled the collar of her cloak up against the wind, and looked back at the bright lake beside which she had lived and died, so long and often. Far below was the house, dwarfed now. Little shots, rifle and revolver fire, drifted up to her, and were snatched away by the wind and distance. Her eyes filled with tears. Then she turned and rode away.

The leader of the Exterminators rose from his work and looked about him. He put his hand to his mouth and called.

"Zed!"

There was no reply, except for a few scattered shots that echoed through the trees.

"Zed!" He turned and called again, in a new direction. "Zed!"

He called out to his leader to all the points of the compass, north, east, south, and west. He must be near. If he was still alive. Had he died in opening the wall?

"Zed!"

Zed was enclosed by the thick woods. The crashed head was in front of them. It lay on its side, half buried, the once grotesque mouth now a doorway. It had fallen straight into the wood, not disturbing the outer brush.

No one would suspect it was here. He took Consuella into the mouth, into the cavern that had brought him here.

While the Exterminators looted and destroyed that which they could never understand, Zed comforted Consuella. They could hide safely here until the storm had passed.

Days later, the last of the soldiers had gone. Zed ventured out for food and soon returned. This was their home.

They lived as one, through many seasons, Consuella bearing him a son, who grew and left them – a single voyager, going out into the light, perhaps to meet May's children.

Zed and Consuella grew old together. Death took them, then time took their bones into dust, until all that remained was his gun, rusting beside a handprint on the rock.

INTERVIEW WITH JOHN BOORMAN BY ANTHONY GALLUZZO

Anthony Galluzzo: In the preface to the novelization of *Zardoz*, you ascribe some of the film's visionary intensity to the place where you live in Ireland; "Those ghosts that stalked the Celtic twilight pressing this strange vision of the future upon me," meaning *Zardoz*. What would you say is the exact relationship between the Wicklow Hills, the Celtic twilight, and the film, the novel.

John Boorman: Well, for me, living fifty-three years in this house in Wicklow, I have become very entwined with Irish legend, which is both from the past and from the future. And *Zardoz* is a vision of the future, which I hope never comes. So there is a kind of tension there.

AG: One of the most difficult tasks in writing a book about the film was to summarize the plot. It's a very strange, baroque, sort of surrealist science-fiction film that really departs from what I call hyper-modernist science-fiction movies like *Star Trek* or *2001*, which came out only a few years before *Zardoz*

JB: I write the story, go to my agent in Los Angeles, ask him to get me some money to make it. He's having this conversation with the head of the studio, who said to him, "Look, explain it to me and I'd be glad to make it, but you have to tell me what it's about." So my agent said, "Not on the phone, face-to-face over a desk, not on the phone," evading the question. My story seemed to be unwelcome and not espoused by the studio heads.

AG: I know that Jeffrey Unsworth, who did some of the camera work on *2001*, also shot *Zardoz*. Would you say that *Zardoz* is partly a response to films like *2001*? That movie very explicitly folds visions of technological mastery into a religious view of transcendence, of how human beings are going to transcend the body and time and our animal natures. It seems in *Zardoz* you're really pushing against that in terms of the story and also the visuals.

JB: Stanley [Kubrick] was a very rational person, and in *2001* he succeeded in going beyond his rationalism, you know; he somehow overcame his rationality and became gracious. And it was great art, it was a great masterpiece.

In *Zardoz* you are taken to a world beyond *2001*, and the reader and the viewer have to allow themselves to be taken into a strange dimension and to not expect to understand it, but to – I hope – *experience* it. That's my wish, but I would say that *Zardoz* comes directly out of Stanley Kubrick's imagination.

AG: It really is in some ways like the perfect counterpoint to

2001. It's really one of the most visually distinctive films I've ever seen.

JB: Yes. Well, I was following a dream, really. It's a dream inspired by *2001*, but it went further. The thing that was unsatisfactory about *2001* was the ending, and in *Zardoz* I was providing *2001* with a superior ending, in all modesty.

AG: Unlike the end of *2001*, *Zardoz* is not about transcending our creaturely condition. To a certain extent, it's about, the fact that we're embodied beings. So it seems like it's in the service of a very different philosophical vision than *2001*.

JB: That's right. Well, you have to recall, the film *2001* – and presumably the book – was a failure in the sense that it didn't really connect. When the film came out it failed, really, but it set up a large body of correspondence, which brought endless questions about it, which I attempted to answer. And it still has, throughout the world, an enormous number of admirers who look upon it as almost this sacred text.

AG: It seems like one of the things you're doing is satirizing the self-seriousness and pretensions of a certain kind of science-fiction film, and you were using elements like bathos and the Grotesque and the Carnivalesque in the service of that satire. Was that deliberate?

JB: Yes, I love that too. But we have to be careful about our love. Keep it secret. Pretend we're doing something else.

AG: It seems like there's also a lot of literature in *Zardoz*. I know you mentioned in a couple of interviews [Aldous] Huxley's work *After Many a Summer Dies the Swan.* I see a lot of Swift, *Gulliver's Travels*, and the island of Laputa. Did you have literary influences at the time that informed the film?

JB: Well, I read quite a lot of fiction at that time. I was very interested in versions of the future. I read a number of science-fiction books about that. I was just reading whatever science fiction was around at the time. I think Kubrick gave a sense of importance to science fiction then.

I knew Stanley quite well, but mostly our relationship was telephonic. We spoke nearly every day. I went out to dinner with him once, and it was the only time I saw him in the flesh. And the interesting thing is that, when we came out from the dinner, his Mercedes was parked there, and he flashed it with his hand, you know, to open the doors, and he showed me, with some pride, that he could open the doors of the Mercedes at a distance. Every production car in America opened the doors like that.

Because I'd made a film in South America, he said to me, "Have you seen the cinema down there, in South America. All the American films have subtitles, it's ridiculous. Half the people down there can't read." So he *said 2001* should be dubbed. So this is part of his logic, you know? I'd been to and sat in cinemas in South America, and they have one man who can read, and he reads the subtitles over to the crowd that's sitting there.

So Stanley said, "No, I'm going to dub it." He dubbed it and the film completely failed because, you know, a dubbed film is a South American film in their eyes, they're not going to bother to see it. And Stanley, you know, thought he could run the world from his telephone, and he missed a lot of important issues like that.

What do you think of his film?

AG: I like his films; they're very cold and clinical. One difference is that *2001* and then *A Clockwork Orange* were adaptations, but *Zardoz* is an original piece. I was trained as a literary scholar, so for my book *Against the Vortex* I spent a lot of time on the novel that you wrote with Bill Stair.

JB: Of course, a lot of the ideas came from Bill Stair. He had the madness of an original, a continuous flow of ideas, mostly untrainable, really.

I admired him greatly. He went mad, you know; couldn't do anything about him. He thought his wife, his employers, all of them, were plotting to put him in a lunatic asylum. So one day he went down to the lunatic asylum, knocked on the door, and said, "I know my family and employers have been trying to get me down here, and I know they've been plotting with you, and I've decided to give myself up," and he was very, very disappointed they wouldn't take him in.

AG: What was it like to film a kind of satire against all this big, grandiose science fiction from the perspective of a quite small, stripped-down, but nonetheless very intense vision of the future?

JB: Well, it certainly tested the imaginations of the studio heads, to the extent that they couldn't really follow it. I had great difficulty getting the money, and I didn't get enough money, really. I did make it to film on a fairly low budget, but I was determined to make it and somehow managed to do it.

AG: But you managed to get these big stars. Sean Connery: Wasn't *Zardoz* his first movie after leaving the James Bond franchise?

JB: He loved doing it, Sean. He loved doing it. And he loved the fact that it took him further away from Bond than you could possibly imagine. He thought when he was doing the Bonds that he was a servant with a mask, with a master who was very severe. And I think doing my film was the first time he got out of Bond.

AG: And yet the character of Zed is almost like a very strange, satirical depiction of Bond, right? He finds out is that he's been effectively killing his own people to serve the agenda of this elite that exists behind these high walls.

JB: I suppose, yes, you could say that. But the key is the last speech, when they're all saying how they had invented these ideas, and he says, "I have looked into the face of the force that put the idea in your mind."

AG: One of the things that comes up in the film is this idea of "the gift of death." The people within the Vortex, the Eternals, they're effectively immortal, they're like gods. And they're miserable.

JB: Yeah, the attempt to make a perfect society has failed, hasn't it? Because, you know, they live forever, but they have to mete out punishment and so forth. You know, one of the best scenes in the film is when Sean Connery sees the dying man and he says – when he's released from living forever – "A good death." That's one of my [favourite] scenes.

AG: I know that the story of *Zardoz* was initially very different. Originally the story was about a hippie girl who disappeared into the communes of Northern California and her professor, I think, is pursuing her, and it was only set a few years in the future. Then that developed into *Zardoz*.

JB: Yes, well it developed over the course of our inventing it, and there was a response to everything that was happening. That was what I felt was the intention, really: taking things that were happening and projecting them into the future. So I think that *Zardoz* has a connection with the present that often science fiction doesn't have.

AG: I think the movie is prophetic. There was a certain

segment of the counterculture that ended up growing into what we know as Silicon Valley. And now we have these people, the Elon Musks and the Peter Thiels who are talking about the singularity. They want to merge with supercomputers like the Tabernacle, and they're very interested in immortality. They talk about how the Earth has been destroyed so we'll just leave the Earth and settle Mars.

JB: Well, this seems to be the only planet where the air is at 21 percent oxygen. And that's some kind of miracle, really. Nowhere else has it as far as we know, as far as we've explored the universe. This seems to be the only planet in the galaxy that animals and human beings can all stay alive on. And that's the miracle of this planet.

AG: The film also engages with what we call the environmental crisis, with a lot of the debates about population, about the environment.

JB: Yes, certainly. That was in all our minds at that time, wasn't it? It seemed overpopulation was going to be the big issue, and it has gone on and now India is the most populous country. It seems to be possible, India and these other places, sustaining large populations. But I think the moment will soon come when there just isn't enough to go around.

AG: I mean, would you say that *Zardoz* is a political film in a way?

JB: Well, I suppose so. I mean, I was a left-wing radical at the time, and I think some of those views found their way into the text of *Zardoz*.

AG: I've heard that the Brutals were predominantly played by local people from the traveling community.

JB: Yes. I'm afraid that's true. It was easier to make it in Ireland, than it would've been in the UK, because the Irish have the ability to extend and open their imaginations, you know? And it was a pleasure to make it.

REPEATER BOOKS

is dedicated to the creation of a new reality. The landscape of twenty-first-century arts and letters is faded and inert, riven by fashionable cynicism, egotistical self-reference and a nostalgia for the recent past. Repeater intends to add its voice to those movements that wish to enter history and assert control over its currents, gathering together scattered and isolated voices with those who have already called for an escape from Capitalist Realism. Our desire is to publish in every sphere and genre, combining vigorous dissent and a pragmatic willingness to succeed where messianic abstraction and quiescent co-option have stalled: abstention is not an option: we are alive and we don't agree.